# Table of Contents

# Mated to a Mage

The Nightshade Guild Series

Book One

USA Today Bestselling Author

## Cassidy K. O'Connor

Mated to a Mage
©Copyright 2021 Cassidy K. O'Connor
Published by: Celtic Hearts Press, LLC
Cover by: B Creative Designs
Formatting by: Celtic Hearts Press, LLC

# Dedication

To my boys... whose love of anime sparks their creativity enough to bring me exciting plots and characters. I'll always be grateful to them for their willingness to sit and talk storylines with me for hours. Who would have thought two boys who hate to read and write would be so good at creating worlds with me!

# Chapter One

I sla Ryan had seen thousands of sunrises and they never ceased to make her misty-eyed. She sat on the bench that she had carved from a fallen tree at the edge of the cliff overlooking the Atlantic Ocean. She had no fear of the water being four hundred feet below her. The beauty of her home in Doolin, Ireland was unlike any other place she had visited in her two hundred and ten years of life.

She closed her eyes and absorbed the power she gained from the rising sun.

Goosebumps ran up her arms causing her to jump up. The magical perimeter set around her home alerted her someone had crossed the border. She grabbed the coffee cup she had brought with her and made the short walk back to her cottage. She relaxed as she saw who her visitor was. Saria was an Elf who lived at the Elven court. They'd been friends for years but rarely saw each other. She smiled and waved, then rushed forward when she saw the look on the girl's face. "What's happened?"

The silver-haired beauty wiped a tear from her face, and her chin quivered as she tried to control her breathing. "The King and Queen are dead. They were assassinated last night in their sleep."

Isla held her arms out and wrapped the girl in a tight hug. "I'm so sorry. What of the bairn?"

Saria stepped out of her embrace. "Princess Ameria survived, the council is in an uproar. They've requested the Nightshade Guild's presence as soon as possible."

Isla nodded quickly. "Of course, I'll summon them now." She held her hand up and touched the small circular tattoo on her left wrist. It was the emblem of the Nightshade Guild and also how they reached out to each other. Some members of the Guild were only able to teleport when summoned via the tattoo.

The emblem glowed golden as she closed her eyes and whispered *tar chugam*. Even though it was in her native Irish tongue, her magic translated her message for them, *come to me*.

She opened her eyes and nodded to the Elf waiting anxiously. "Tis done, they'll be here momentarily."

A shimmer in the yard crystalized as the first three mages appeared. She wasn't surprised Morwen Rowe was so quick, she was nearby in

Scotland. Finnegan Padrick in all his six-foot six glory stood next to her. Slightly shorter but still a giant to Isla stood Cale Cawthorn; their only Guild member who chose to live in literal Hell rather than among mortals.

A second later Lena Graves and her cat familiar, Hex, popped into view along with Jemma Blackwood, Sunny Burson, Demi Mephisto, and Serena Moon, whose glisten of wet hair indicated she may have been summoned mid-swim.

Finnegan glanced down at Hex. "I see his hair still hasn't grown back in?"

Lena huffed. "Don't mention it in front of him. He still hasn't completely forgiven me."

Isla didn't know who she felt worse for, the cat who had a firebolt accidentally sent his way or Lena whose powers were glitchy and accidentally burned the hair off the cat's tail.

The next to appear was Charlotte "Charlie" Nocker. It was the middle of the night in Oklahoma and Charlie was a baker so she would have gotten up in a few hours anyway.

Morwen's shoulders slumped slightly. "You didn't bring any goodies for us?"

Charlie shrugged. "It took everything I had to wake up enough to remember to put on clothes. I promise to bring some next time."

The group chuckled as they looked around and saw which mages still hadn't shown.

Cale sighed. "Why am I not surprised those two are last?"

Arion popped into view, yawning as he waved to the group. Isla didn't really blame him for his odd sleep schedule. He was a rock star on tour. He'd probably only been asleep an hour when she called.

Last to arrive was Nicoletta "Nic" Dean with her hedgehog Franklin on her shoulder. "There had better be a really good reason for waking me up this early."

Isla waved at Saria. "We've been summoned by the Elven council. The King and Queen were assassinated last night."

Her announcement perked Nic and Arion up immediately, both going from a slouch to a wide-awake, shoulders back stance. The Guild murmured to each other, everyone understood the gravity of the situation and how it went well beyond the Elven kingdom.

Saria waved her hand as she whispered a chant. A swirling mist of colors opened in front of them. "This will take us straight to the council."

Isla opened her front door and whistled. Her familiar Brayan wasn't much of a morning creature, so while she enjoyed the sunrise, he'd stayed sleeping in bed. The tiny animal bounded into view chittering with excitement when he saw the other mages. "Sorry, they're not here for a visit. We have somewhere to be."

She bent down and picked up the Irish Stoat and set it on her shoulder. She loved the animal to the ends of the earth and would gladly obliterate anyone who offended him by calling him a weasel or ferret.

Isla nodded to Saria, then waited her turn to walk through the portal. With her stomach in knots, knowing they were going to discuss the murder of two people she knew well and the grief she had no doubt she would feel if she saw the orphaned princess, her heart broke for the ten-month-old whose life just got a whole lot more complicated.

# Chapter Two

I sla stepped through the portal and into an ornate hallway lined in gold. Cale grabbed his chest and moaned. Isla rubbed his back. "Tis that bad?"

He took a deep breath. "I have my wards up right now but there is so much grief and fear it's overwhelming."

Isla felt for him, the Elven kingdom was a terrible place for an empath to be at that moment.

Sunny walked up. It was strange to not see her trademark smile. "I'd offer to walk around and see if I could heal some of their pain but I think there's too many."

Saria strolled up to the double doors a few feet away. "The council doesn't want anyone knowing you are here, so it's best if you stay with me."

Isla quirked her eyebrow at her friend. It was a strange request that they stay hidden. Surely anyone in the Elven kingdom would be glad to have the Nightshade Guild offer their assistance.

The group filed into the room and stood shoulder-to-shoulder taking in the sight before them. The thirteen elders of the Elven council stood around a giant oak table arguing with each other. Saria shut the door hard enough to catch their attention. They immediately closed their mouths and sat down. Why they tried to act like the Guild hadn't witnessed their meltdown made zero sense to Isla but elves were a proud race.

Nic's father, Klaus, waved to his daughter before wiping the smile from his face. "Thank you all for coming on such short notice. Sometime in the early morning hours, someone snuck into King Theoden and Queen Syllia's chamber and pierced their hearts with a dagger." His voice hitched as he continued on, "We believe the assassin then went to Princess Ameria's chamber to either assassinate or kidnap her but must have gotten startled and left without completing the task. We found blood on the side of the crib and on the windowsill of her room."

The elder to his right spoke up, his voice shaking in anger. "Only an Elf could have gotten to both chambers without any guards seeing them or suspecting anything strange. It had to have been an inside job."

Klaus shook his head angrily. "It doesn't make sense. Only the ones who wear the crown can control the magic. They wouldn't have wanted to kill Ameria. That would send the Kingdom into even greater turmoil. They had to have been trying to steal her but I don't know why any Elf would do that to their own people."

The ancient-looking woman next to him fisted her hands on the table. "That is why we've called you here. We trust the Guild to be impartial and to keep the balance of the supernatural world. We'd like you to hide the princess until we've found the assassin and rooted out anyone involved in their plan."

Isla's eyes widened but she resisted glancing at her fellow mages. They were likely as shocked as she was.

Jemma raised her hand to get everyone's attention. "Remind me again how old the child is?"

It was a fair question but Isla knew the real reason Jemma asked was because she wasn't fond of children.

Klaus answered. "She is ten months old and starting to come into her powers early. We have no doubt she will be as strong or stronger than her parents were." The council beamed with pride at his proclamation before their grief engulfed them again.

The female Elf continued. "We do have one stipulation though. We only want her in the company of one of you at a time and for no longer than a month." She held her hand up to silence them before they could argue. "I'm happy to list our reasoning. Most importantly we don't want anyone getting complacent or dependent on another and put the child at risk. We have no doubt once word gets out about the assassination, the entire supernatural world will be hunting for her. Everyone will want control of the future Elf queen and the magic she will rule over. We also don't want her getting too attached to any of you. She needs to have a smooth transition back to court when we're ready for her to come home."

Isla had to admit their logic was sound. Regardless of whether she agreed, you didn't argue with an Elf. They were infuriatingly stubborn.

She finally glanced up and down the line. They had a decision to make, did they risk upending the supernatural world by not helping, or did they agree to care for an infant for an undetermined length of time while being hunted day and night?

She turned back to the council. "We need a minute to speak alone."

The Guild stood in silence as the council filed out of the room through a door behind their table. Saria smiled at Isla before closing the door. The girl had hope written all over her face. Isla already knew what they had to do, whether they wanted to or not.

# Chapter Three

The Guild formed a circle but didn't say a word. They studied each other's faces, everyone trying to absorb everything they were told, and what the ramifications were if they did or didn't help.

Jemma broke the silence first. "I have no idea how to take care of a baby. This sounds like a nightmare."

Cale nodded. "I have no doubt I could handle a baby and I think we absolutely do need to help but I need time to prepare. There's no way I'm taking her down to Hell with me, so I'll need to make arrangements."

Arion held his hand up. "I'm on tour until the holidays so if we do this, I'd like to request I take the last shift. No child needs to see what happens backstage at a concert."

The group chuckled; they had all heard stories

of his escapades on the road.

Nic sighed. "I'm not thrilled at the idea of a baby waking me up at whatever ungodly hour but I request not to take the first shift. We don't know if the assassin is going to strike again, I want to make sure my father is safe."

Sunny's bright smile had returned. "I think having a baby around sounds like fun but it's the dead of winter in Alaska right now. I should probably take her when it warms up more."

One by one the rest spoke up and it became quite clear no one was offering to take the child first. Isla crossed her arms, unconsciously comforting herself. She had very little interaction with children and the fears of inadequacy were threatening to overwhelm her. "Fine, I get it, I'll take the first shift."

Nic patted her on the shoulder. "I'll take her after you."

Isla nodded. "At the end of the month, I'll contact you to agree on a meeting place."

Cale held his hand up to stop Isla as she turned to make her way toward the door the council had gone through. "Not yet. I trust all of you with my life but we're talking about the person who controls the flow of all Elven magic. I believe we're all above temptation, however, I think we should perform a binding spell. Each of us will swear to protect the Princess with their life until she is returned to the Kingdom. It will take all surviving members to undo the bond so she can be returned."

Isla held her hand out, palm up. She had no qualms with doing the spell. She had already decided she would give her life for the child's if needed.

One by one the rest held their hands out, palms up. As one they began to chant. "With this oath, I pledge to protect Princess Ameria Dormaris at all cost. She will be safe with the Guild until she is returned to her homeland."

A symbol of the crown of the royal family appeared like a tattoo in the center of their palms then absorbed into the skin as if it were never there.

Isla made eye contact with each mage waiting for their nod of agreement before walking over to the door and opening it for the council to come back in.

The elves returned to their seats and waited. Isla ignored the nerves squirming through her belly as she addressed them. They were not going to like what she had to say. "We've agreed to your request. To be absolutely sure the Princess is safe, we won't give you the schedule." She held her hands up to stop them as soon as they started to grumble in protest. "We're sure none of you are behind the assassination, however, we don't know. Hopefully, you agree it's safest for no one but us to know where she is?" The council reluctantly agreed. "We'll reach out to you for periodic updates on your search."

Saria opened the door behind the council and waved Gorman in. Isla felt for the King's brother. He looked ragged. The man had lost his wife tragically a few months earlier and now his brother.

Tucked in his arms was the golden-haired beauty. The Princess looked like a porcelain doll complete with rosy lips and sparkling green eyes that swirled like leaves in the wind. Isla was glad her thick curls would help hide the girl's pointy ears. She didn't want to use any of her magic unless necessary and keeping up a glamour on someone for an entire month would take its toll.

Gorman's eyes were full of tears as he passed the baby off to Isla, then handed over a giant duffel bag. Ameria gazed at Isla and smiled, a tiny bit of drool threatening to run down her chin. "Maybe this won't be so bad."

The words were barely out of her mouth when the Princess hiccupped, then spit-up. Vile smelling white liquid came out of her mouth. Isla shot a panicked look to Saria but the young girl shrugged unapologetically and opened a portal. This was going to be the longest month of Isla's life.

Isla was the last mage to step through the portal, and it closed immediately behind her. The Guild stood in a circle staring at her, no one had words.

Lena grabbed her cell phone out of her pocket and held it up. "I'm going to work on the app I created for us to communicate with each other. I want to make sure it's completely secure and if someone were to kill one of us and get our phones, they wouldn't be able to use them to track the rest of the Guild."

Arion cast his eyes down toward the floor and mumbled. "God, you're dark sometimes."

Lena shrugged. "I'll do what I must to protect you all."

Isla smiled at the younger girl. "You're the best hacker we know, we are grateful for any extra protection you can give us."

Lena slid her phone back into her pocket. "I'll be in touch with each of you when the updates are ready." She touched the tattoo on her wrist and disappeared.

The ever-optimistic Sunny walked over and patted Isla's shoulder. "I'm sure you're going to have a great time with this little munchkin. Good luck and call if you need anything." She rubbed the baby's cheek then disappeared.

One by one the rest of the Guild gave their condolences before teleporting away.

Nic blew out a heavy breath. "Well, this has to be the strangest assignment we've ever had."

Isla switched the baby to her other arm, surprised how quickly her muscles got tired. "The one with the highest stakes as well. I don't know if I'll be able to stay here or if I'll have to keep moving. I'll reach out to you when it's time to hand her off."

Nic nodded as she pressed the tattoo on her wrist and disappeared from view.

Isla gazed at the baby staring up at her. "Well, it's just you and me now kid."

A loud fart vibrated against her arm followed by the smell of death. "Shit."

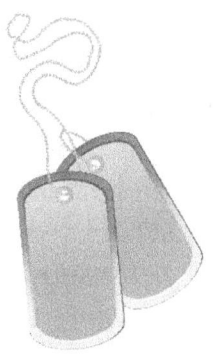

# Chapter Four

**K**illian Stewart stood at the tree line watching the cliffs. Two months ago, he had discovered the overlook and the woman who sat there every morning enjoying the sunrise. Was it creepy he watched her every day? Probably. Did that stop him? Nope. He wasn't doing anything wrong.

He wasn't in a good place in his life and didn't need to drag her into it. He couldn't deny though there was something about her that kept drawing him to her. He tried to stay away but couldn't.

The bench she usually sat on was empty, the sun already rising high in the sky. He likely had missed her and it was all his stupid PTSD's fault. The previous night had been New Year's Eve and the fireworks were jarring enough to trigger nightmares. When sleep had finally come to him, it was deep enough to keep him asleep way past his normal time.

He still felt raw from the previous night's episode and didn't want to return to his empty cottage rental so soon. With a heavy sigh, he walked to her bench and sat. Fresh footsteps in the mud meant he hadn't missed her by much. He stared out over the water and wondered what she thought about each morning as she sat there. Did she have some big life trauma she was trying to cope with like he did? Did she just enjoy nature and think this was the best place to savor it? She always left there with a smile on her face and a bounce in her step. Maybe if he sat there long enough, he would feel a little less broken.

It had been two days and she still hadn't come to the cliffs. After doing the same routine for fifty-eight straight days it seemed out of character for her to not show up. There were very few cottages in this area of Ireland, which is why he had picked it for his sabbatical. On one of his first hikes, he had passed the closest cottage and saw her standing on her porch plucking herbs and flowers from several potted plants. It was freezing outside but she stood in a tank top and sweatpants as if it were the middle of summer. He found it fascinating that she was a tiny woman living in a cottage in the middle of nowhere, covered in tattoos, and looked ready to take on the world.

She had a story and he really wanted to know what it was.

The sun was shining bright, and still, she hadn't shown. He was a military man, routine was everything to him. He needed to make sure she was fine. Ignoring the idea, he would look like a stalker he decided to take a leisurely hike by her place and see if everything was in order.

Thanks to his many years in the service, he was in the best shape of his life. He quickly made the short walk to her cottage without breaking a sweat. As the house came into view, he heard a squishing sound. The noise had come from his shoes sinking into the mud. It hadn't rained in days. As he broke through the tree line encircling her house, he paused and gaped at the sky. A large black storm cloud hovered above the cottage, rain poured down, drenching everything. The yard was flooded, the water almost level with the bottom step of the porch. "What the hell?" He grumbled as he walked back a few paces and confirmed there were no other storm clouds as far as he could see.

He sloshed his way back to the edge of her yard and studied the house. He wanted to make sure she was okay then he'd be on his way. It was the neighborly thing to do, even if she had no clue he was a neighbor.

As he took his first step onto the porch, a new sound reached his ears. He closed his eyes and focused on the noises. It sounded like a baby screaming and a woman crying and begging it to stop. As he neared the door, an intense feeling of sadness washed over him.

He'd had no intention of actually interacting with her, but every fiber of his being was demanding he knock. He straightened his clothes and combed his fingers through his hair. "There's nothing to worry about. Just say you were walking by and heard some noise and wanted to make sure she was okay. That will sound innocent enough." The pep talk did little to make him feel better. He cleared his throat and knocked loudly.

The door creaked open; the woman stood there with a screaming child on her hip. She had deep bags under her eyes, her magenta hair looked like it hadn't been brushed in days, and there was a brown streak on her cheek that he hoped was chocolate and not something much worse.

"Aye, how did ye get here?" The girl looked past him then down at the baby. "It's ye isn't it, yer making me so crazy I didna hear the warning of a trespasser."

*She had perimeter alarms?* He was impressed that she took her safety so seriously. She set the baby on the ground and pushed past him. He watched as she marched from one end of the porch to the other studying the woods.

Killian cleared his throat to get her attention. "I'm your neighbor. I was hiking and heard the baby crying. I wanted to make sure everything was fine."

The tiny woman walked past him back into the

house and started pacing. He stood at the entrance not wanting to scare her by going in without permission. Although she didn't seem the least bit worried about the six-foot-three, well-built stranger standing in her doorway.

She talked to herself as if she were alone. "If a human can get to the door without me knowing, who knows what else could. With all that rain someone likely picked up on the disturbance."

*Human? Were animals such a threat in the area? And if so, why hadn't he been warned?* He made a mental note to check in with his landlord when he got back to the rental.

The tiny, screaming bundle at his feet was starting to fray his nerves. The woman was still oblivious to him so he picked up the baby. She stopped crying as she reached up and touched the stubble on his chin. A high-pitched giggle rang through the cottage. It likely wouldn't have sounded so loud except the rain chose that very moment to stop. Without the water pounding on the roof and against the windows, the house was suddenly silent.

The woman froze and spun in their direction. "How did ye do that?" Killian stared at her, not sure what she was asking. "I've been tryin' to get her to sleep fer two days and all she's done is cry."

He didn't have an answer for her because he hadn't done anything. He knew very little about kids but he could sense the baby just wanted to be comforted. Her head full of golden curls laid against his chest. He rubbed her back a few times and watched her eyes close.

"Ye wee fecker." Killian may be American but even he got the gist of what she just said. "Thank ye for gettin' her to sleep. If ye could lay her in her cot it would be appreciated."

He glanced around and saw a crib next to the couch. Assuming that's what a cot was, he laid the baby down and walked back over to the door. "Anyway, like I was saying, I happened to be passing by."

The young woman touched his shoulder and turned him towards the door. "Many thanks, now off with ye."

She closed the door on his back. Killian stood there with his jaw dropped. He had no idea what had just happened but it was obvious she had dismissed him. Unsure what else to do, he decided to go home and call his landlord. It was time he found out if there were animals in the forest he needed to be worried about and maybe he'd casually ask if they knew the sexy neighbor who hadn't even looked at him twice.

# Chapter Five

Isla rushed around her cabin thinking of everything she might need while on the run for the next twenty-six days. If a human could get past her wards without her knowing, that meant anything could and that wasn't a risk she could take. It was obvious the Elf child was manipulating her emotions. She was glad she'd chosen an earlier shift, the older the child got the stronger she was going to be. Isla felt bad for the mages who would go last. They were going to have their hands full.

She grabbed a satchel and mumbled a spell so the inside of the bag was limitless. She tossed vials of potions, crystals, and clothes inside then turned back to the sleeping child.

Isla whistled for Brayan who climbed on her shoulder then gently lifted Ameria out of the cot and made her way to the door. She gave her place one last look. She had strengthened all of her protection spells in the hopes that her home would still be there when she got back. If anyone suspected the Guild of having the baby, they would have no qualms about burning everything to the ground until they found her.

This was the first time in her life she wished she had a car. With a sigh of resignation, she trudged through the mud and began the walk into the closest town. She didn't have a plan yet except to keep moving.

After a few yards, the back of her neck tingled. She wasn't alone. She closed her eyes, sensing who or what was around her. "I know you're there, come out."

She stopped and waited. The sexy American who had been watching her for the last couple of months walked out from behind a tree. She never minded him spying on her before. His aura made it clear he lusted after her and a quick dip into his mind showed he had no ill intent toward her. When she had been poking around in his head, she'd seen intense pain and retreated immediately. She wasn't going to probe where she didn't belong. It was obvious to her he was hurting, so if watching her for a few minutes each day helped him, she didn't mind.

He wiped his hands on his pants nervously. She stayed silent enjoying his discomfort. "I'm not stalking you; I swear. I was really worried about you."

At the sound of his voice, Ameria woke up. Isla groaned in frustration. She did not want to hike in the pouring rain, which happened whenever the child was upset. Ameria reached for the American and fussed. Black clouds formed overhead.

Isla let out a resigned huff. "I appreciate yer concern but we're fine. A storm's coming, ye should get home."

Ameria let out a screech of anger that the man hadn't taken her, her hands opened and closed rapidly as she reached for him. Thunder rumbled nearby. He held his hands up. "I have nothing going on, if you don't mind company, I can hold her and walk with you?"

Isla glanced at the rapidly swelling clouds. "Can it be?" She handed the child to the man and watched the sky clear immediately. "Ye wee git. How's that for thanks? I didn't have ta take ye in ye know?"

Ameria smiled at Isla then burrowed against the stranger's chest. He cleared his throat. "Um, not to pry but does that mean you aren't her mother?"

Isla studied him for a second. If he could control the child's emotions, she would have a much easier time keeping her safe. Maybe it wouldn't hurt to keep him around for a bit. "My name is Isla Ryan; the child's mum and dad are unwell so I'm keepin' her fer awhile."

The man glanced at the baby in his arms and then back to her. "I'm sorry to hear that. She must be missing them terribly. I'm Killian Stewart, here on vacation."

Isla motioned for him to walk with her. "So, what do ye do in America that makes ye such a baby whisperer?"

Killian shrugged. "Honestly, I just left the Marines. Kids are a pretty foreign concept to me."

Isla studied the child. *Why was the Princess drawn to a man she didn't know?* Elves were known for their glimpses into the future. This was a ten-month-old baby though. Did she really know something Isla and Killian didn't?

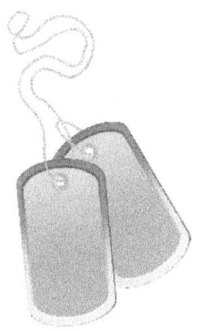

# Chapter Six

*W*hat the hell am I doing? Killian couldn't believe he'd gotten himself into this situation. He stopped by for his daily dose of seeing her, and suddenly he's joining her for an outing and somehow keeping the baby happy. This was definitely the weirdest day of his life. When he'd asked the landlord about her the guy had mumbled something about a nice girl that kept to herself then changed the subject. He also said there were zero animals to be worried about. That only intrigued Killian more. What could she be trying to protect herself from?

Killian noticed the backpack and duffel bag strapped to Isla's back. "I know I don't have a lot of experience with babies but that seems like a lot of baggage for something so tiny."

"Ye have no idea," Isla grumbled. "We're actually going on a trip, we'll be gone fer a couple of weeks." He glanced at the baby then back at Isla. She chuckled. "I'm aware how much this may suck but I'm confident this wee one and I will make it work."

She reached for the baby, who immediately started to fuss and pull away.

Killian gave them a cheesy smile. "I guess I have the magic touch."

Isla scowled at him. A roar echoed through the trees.

Killian tensed. "What the hell? They said there were no big animals around here."

Isla's eyes rounded. Fear etched across her face. "Run."

Without question, he held tight to the baby and took off. He stayed one step behind Isla making sure she was in his sight at all times. Twigs snapped and leaves crunched behind them but they didn't stop running until they reached the back of a few buildings. They squeezed between them and popped out on the main road.

People stopped and stared at them as they gasped for air.

Isla grabbed his arm and dragged him across the street into a restaurant. The bell over the door rang as they entered. The patrons were oblivious to the fact that they had just run for their lives.

Isla smiled at the hostess. "Table for three please."

Killian glanced out the door expecting to see a bear tearing through the streets. People milled about, carrying on about their normal day. Isla reached back and touched his arm. "Come along."

He followed her to a table in the back corner. She hung the bags from a chair then sat. Out of habit he moved to the opposite side and tried to take the chair facing the door so he could watch the entrance.

Isla lunged toward him and stopped him. "Ye can't sit there, you'll crush poor Brayan."

Killian stared at the empty chair then back at Isla. She was dead serious and he was too confused to question it. He pointed to the chair across from her. "Is this seat available?" He already knew the answer.

She quirked an eyebrow at him. "Ye can clearly see that it is."

He shook his head as he sat across from her. He was starting to think she had a few loose screws and wasn't sure it was safe to leave the baby with her.

He turned Ameria around and sat her on his lap. She immediately reached for the silverware. "Oh no, you don't."

Isla dug into the bag behind her then set a bottle of milk on the table. The baby squealed as she grabbed it and leaned back against his chest and drank it.

Isla shook her head. "Unbelievable. Ye got some power over her." She leaned forward and stared intently into his eyes. "Tell me again why ye came to my house?"

He groaned. If he repeated the story, she may think he was a creep. With no other choice, he told her again. "I was walking by. I heard the baby crying and you didn't sound like you were having a very good time. On top of that, your yard was flooded from rain that was only over your house. Curiosity got the best of me so I knocked."

She slowly tapped her fingernails on the table.

He glanced away and sighed. "Okay, fine. I've seen you up at the cliffs a few times. You didn't show up for a couple of days and I wanted to know why."

A waiter walked up, breaking the tension of his admission. "Hello, my name is Geoff and I'll be yer server. Can I get ye a drink?"

Isla smiled at the teenager. "A Guinness fer me."

Killian nodded. "I'll have the same."

Isla watched the boy leave then turned back to Killian. "I knew ye were watchin' me. It was more than a few times though."

His face heated knowing he'd been caught. "If you knew I was there why didn't you ever confront me?"

She shrugged.

Killian was speechless. He was attracted to an unstable woman who liked the idea of him stalking her. The warning bells were going off in his head.

That wasn't going to stop him though. She intrigued him and he had nothing to lose by spending a bit more time with her.

# Chapter Seven

Isla watched Ameria sitting contentedly on Killian's lap. The child obviously wanted him with them and he was alone and a soldier. She had a crazy idea. "Let me see yer hand." He held his arm out, she reached for it and wrapped her hand around his forearm. She closed her eyes and whispered. *"Cuardaitheoir anam."* The rune tattooed on the back of her neck burned as the magic awakened. She searched his soul, saw anger, and devastation. There was so much loneliness from years in the military. He knew nothing of the supernatural world or that there was anything magical about her or the baby.

Her eyes fluttered open as the bell over the door rang. She stiffened at the sight of four werewolves in their human form searching the restaurant. Didn't they know all mages had the sight to see through their disguises? "Bloody eejits."

Killian turned to look around. "What's wrong?"

She squeezed his arm. "I'll grab the bags, calmly follow me." She was relieved that he nodded and didn't question her.

She set a twenty-dollar euro on the table and grabbed the bags. The trio walked toward the hallway leading to the bathrooms. As soon as they were out of sight, she grabbed his hand and whispered. *"Tóg linn."* She felt the familiar drain of magic as she asked the spirits to take them away. In the blink of an eye, they were gone, leaving the werewolves to find nothing but an empty hall.

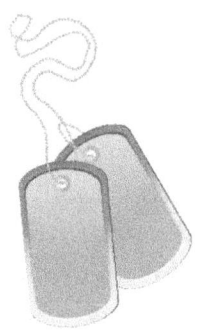

# Chapter Eight

Killian was going to be sick. Whatever Isla was doing to him he wanted to die. When the swirling motion stopped and he was back on solid ground, he bent over and threw up. Lucky for him, he'd had a small breakfast so there wasn't much. He stood up and comforted Ameria who was screaming in his arms. He knew exactly how she felt. He glanced at Isla, dumbfounded that she wasn't sick. "What the hell was that?" He looked behind her and saw they were in an alleyway. "How did we get here?"

She grabbed his hand and pulled him onto the street. "I'll explain soon enough."

He took a deep breath, trying to calm his stomach as he followed her to an Inn across the way.

His legs wobbled as he waited in the lobby

while she went to the check-in desk. A sign posted by the door said they were in Cork. Panic set in. *How the hell are we two hours south of where we just were?*

A whistle across the lobby had him spinning around. Isla stood next to the elevator waving him over. He couldn't figure out how she was so unaffected.

As soon as they were enclosed in the elevator, she slumped against the wall. He finally saw the strain she was under. She was sweating and barely keeping her eyes open. "Are you okay?"

She nodded and straightened up as the doors opened. "I'll be fine."

He followed her to room three nineteen. She held the door open for him and locked it behind them. She walked around the room whispering words he didn't recognize. She walked towards the bed and looked down at it. "Check the hotel, make sure we're safe."

Killian stared at the empty bed. "You want me to check the hotel? For what?"

Isla glanced over her shoulder at him. "Not ye."

Killian let out a deep sigh. "Okay, what the hell is going on? I deserve an answer."

She sat on the edge of the bed. "Yer right ye do but I need a minute." She fell back against the bed.

"Shit." He set Ameria down on the floor and ran to the bed. "Isla, wake up. What's wrong with you?"

The tiny woman in his arms was breathing but out cold. "Well, fuck."

Killian sat in the chair facing the bed. His chin rested on his folded hands as he stared at the woman and child asleep in front of him.

Isla had somehow moved them to a different city then passed out before she could explain. For the first few hours, he swapped between caring for the baby and freaking out about what had happened.

Other than dozing a few times throughout the night, he had stayed awake waiting for her to wake up. He was starting to suspect she was batshit crazy and maybe he was, too.

A gasp from the bed had him jumping to his feet. Isla glanced around frantically until she saw Ameria asleep in the center of a pillow fort he had made on the King-sized bed. She turned back to Killian and smiled shyly. "Ye probably have some questions."

His eyebrows rose until they nearly touched his hairline. "You think?" He paced in front of the bed. "Let's see...something chased us in the woods. Then we somehow moved to a different city, and you talk to an invisible person named Brayan. I can't imagine why I would have questions."

She gently stood up so she didn't move the bed too much. There were still bags under her eyes. He sighed. "I saved you some breakfast." He waved to the small table by the window. He wanted answers but he was willing to give her a minute.

They sat in silence while she ate the fried eggs and toast he'd ordered. He watched her closely and noticed she picked up the now cold cup of tea, whispered something then took a sip. Steam rose from the cup as she put it down. He could imagine the look on his face, it likely mirrored the panic building inside, like when he was on tour and intuition told him to be careful but really there was no visible reason.

Finally, she sat back and crossed her hands in her lap. "After three days of little sleep, teleporting took up most of me magic then warding the room took the rest. I didna mean to fall asleep but I had to regain me strength. I'm grateful to ye fer keeping Ameria safe while I recovered."

"M-m-magic?" He struggled to comprehend what she was saying.

She chuckled as she stood up and walked towards him. "I can give ye the sight. It'll help explain it all."

He froze as her hand reached for him, he didn't know what to expect and wasn't embarrassed to admit a little afraid. She grabbed the chain of his necklace and pulled it from under his shirt. He grabbed her wrist and squeezed. "Don't touch..." He shook his head from the rage that exploded through his body. "I'm sorry. I didn't mean to hurt you."

She glanced at the dog tag but didn't say anything about the other man's name that was on it. He watched as her hand closed around it and she whispered, *"Tabhair radharc dó."*

The necklace fell against his chest, electricity tingled throughout his body. Everything burned, he gritted his teeth against the pain, then it was gone.

He opened his eyes and gasped. Glowing lines crisscrossed around the room. "What in the actual hell?"

# Chapter Nine

I sla realized too late she could have eased Killian into the idea of the supernatural world a little easier. There was no going back now though. She walked to the window and opened the curtain. Killian cautiously stepped forward and peered out.

She pointed across the street at two short, hairy creatures. "That couple walking hand in hand are trolls." She pointed to the opposite corner of the road. "That eight-foot-tall guy is an ogre. Without the sight, ye would see normal humans but now ye can see what people really are." Killian stumbled back. His pupils widened and panic flared in his eyes. "If ye don't want to see the truth all ye have to do is take the necklace off. The power will wear off in a few days unless I keep redoing the spell."

A blur of color ran between his legs. He jumped in the air. "Shit, what is that?"

The tiny brown animal used her clothes to crawl up her side and perch on her shoulder. "This is Brayan. He's an Irish Stoat."

Killian studied the creature. "He looks like a weasel."

Brayan growled and bared his teeth.

Isla tsked. "It's okay, he doesn't know any better." She scratched her familiar's head before looking back at Killian. "He's a wee bit sensitive to being called a weasel or ferret."

Killian pursed his lips as he nodded. "I'm just glad to know you weren't talking to yourself this whole time."

She smiled brightly. "I bet ye thought I was feckin loony."

Killian rubbed the back of his neck. "The thought crossed my mind." Isla enjoyed seeing his discomfort. "So, what are you and does that mean he's your pet?"

Isla and Brayan gasped at the same time. "I'm a Mage and he's me familiar. We're connected mentally and physically." When he didn't react to her statement she went on. "I'm like a witch but much cooler and stronger. Mages and their familiars can feel each other's emotions, speak to each other telepathically, and if one of us gets hurt, the other feels it."

Killian quirked an eyebrow. "He can feel *all* of your emotions?"

Her eyebrows scrunched together, confused where he was going with his question. "I suppose so."

"So, even intimate feelings like when you're with another person?"

Laughter burst from Isla, that wasn't what she was expecting. Brayan gagged and ran down her side and over to the bed. They watched as he turned his back on them and curled up next to Ameria.

Killian shrugged. "It was an honest question. I didn't realize he was such a prude." He walked back over to the window and surveyed the street below them. "I think it's time you filled in the rest of the gaps for me. I'm still finding this hard to believe and facts help me calm down."

Isla sat at the table and sipped her tea. "Well, for starters, Elves are real and she is the most important Elf in the world now." They both glanced at the infant asleep with her thumb in her mouth. "Her parents were the King and Queen of their realm, but a week ago they were assassinated."

Killian's head snapped toward Isla. "I'm sorry, what?"

Isla nodded. "Murdered in their sleep. I'm one of twelve members of the Nightshade Guild. The Elven council asked us to keep the baby hidden while they hunt for the killers."

Killian paced across the room. "So, do you think those were the assassins in the cafe yesterday?"

Isla bit her bottom lip as she contemplated his question. "Nay, it was a pack of werewolves and they were just the start. As word spreads about the murders, paranormals from all over will try to find the babe and control her and the entire Elven kingdom. If that happens, it will be bad fer everyone, including humans." She could see his shoulders tensing with each word she said. "I know ye came here for peace and quiet so I have no right to keep ye with me. Ameria is affecting me emotions, which is affecting me magic so I have to keep moving fer the next twenty-five days until me time is up. I can't teleport ye back to yer home and use up me magic. I'll help ye get home though before we go into hiding."

He glanced at Ameria. "Creatures are going to keep hunting you though, right?"

Isla nodded. "They won't stop until the babe is safely back in her castle."

She stayed silent as he paced the room. Finally, he stopped in front of her. "I swore I'd never go to war again but I don't think I can walk away from this. I may not have magic but I'm good with the Princess. I'm trained in hand-to-hand combat and I have excellent aim with a gun. If you will let me, I'll stay and help with Ameria while you focus on keeping her safe?"

It probably wasn't the right time for it but Isla had to pause and get her body back in control. His words had caused her heart rate to speed up. A gorgeous soldier was offering to be a glorified babysitter and let *her* protect *them*. Patriarchy be damned, this was a man. She cleared her throat. "Tis very generous of ye." She sent up a silent prayer of thanks that he wasn't a shifter or he would be able to smell her lust from a mile away.

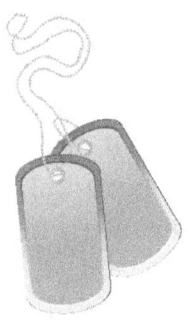

# Chapter Ten

**K**illian wasn't sure what had just happened but the tension in the room had shifted and he didn't know why.

He stared at the beautiful woman in front of him. He'd been wandering for weeks trying to figure out what his purpose in life was now that he was a civilian again. Now he understood. It was his job to help a mage protect a princess. The absurdity of that sentence had him stifling a laugh.

Motion on the bed broke the mood. Isla picked up Ameria. "Good morning, yer highness. Let's get ye changed then some breakfast."

Killian had no practice in diaper changing so he was glad to let her handle it. There was no way he'd make it almost a month without needing to do it, so he walked over and watched.

Once she was clean, Isla handed Ameria out to him. "Can ye hold her while I make her a bottle?"

Ameria giggled as soon as she was in his arms. He'd never had anyone let alone a child react so strongly to him and he wished whatever this power of his was that it would work even a little on Isla. She was beautiful, and strong, and appeared to have zero attraction to him besides as a bodyguard.

He sat at the table and watched Isla grab a silver canister out of a bag. He leaned closer to intently studying every move she made. "The powder was given to me by the Elves. I can add it to any liquid and it will convert it to the nutrients she needs."

"So, the Elf version of human formula."

Isla shrugged. "Yes, but likely much more sophisticated and magical than that."

He grabbed the bottle from Isla and handed it to the baby who leaned against him and drank. "What about your magic, what is your superpower?"

She sat across from him and sipped from her teacup. "There are many types of magic and the mages of the Guild all specialize in at least one kind. I've mastered creation magic. It allows me to temporarily create appendages, buildings, duplicates of myself, Golems, weapons, etc."

Killian's eyes widened. When he was a boy, he had believed in magic but as he got older and saw the harsh reality of the world, he'd stopped believing.

"Tis not all great though. The larger the magic, the more it drains me, like when I needed to sleep after transporting us. I have to fuel every creation so when the magic depletes or I stop focusing on it, the creation disappears. The more creations at one time, the faster I deplete."

Killian smiled broadly, trying to contain his excitement. "That is amazing, so you can create anything you want?"

Isla shook her head. "Nay, I can't create something if I don't understand how it works. Like I know how a car works but not the exact mechanics of an engine so I can't create a working one."

She laid her arm out on the table and pointed at the tattoos. "Nic, one of the other mages, tattoos runes that we can use. It helps amplify a type of magic that we aren't experts in."

Killian let out a deep sigh. "Even with all that power, you don't think you're safe at home?"

Isla's head fell back, she stared at the ceiling before growling. "'Tis better to keep moving. If word got out that I had the child no one within miles of me cabin would be safe. I don't want to have to choose between saving a human and saving the princess."

Killian knew exactly what she meant. Every life was precious but sometimes the needs of the greater good outweighed one person's worth over another. It wasn't fair but war rarely was.

# Chapter Eleven

I sla's eyes fluttered open as the sun came peeking through the curtain. Having Killian there was more comforting than she expected it would be. Once he knew the truth about her, it made it even better. They had spent the rest of the day talking about the supernatural world and what was or wasn't real. When it was time for bed, he demanded she share the bed with the baby while he made a sleeping area out of blankets on the floor between the bed and the hotel room door.

She had laid Ameria next to her and rubbed her back as she sang a lullaby. By the time she was done, she heard deep breathing from Killian.

It had taken her a while to fall asleep, she had warred with herself on whether she was doing the right thing bringing him into the equation. In the end, she trusted her gut and the instincts of the

Princess. She had to believe he was with them for a reason.

The bathroom door creaked open interrupting her musings on the previous evening. She watched as Killian tiptoed out with nothing but a towel around his waist. She stared at the V that disappeared behind the cloth. From his tan skin to his bulging muscles he was perfection. They didn't grow them like that in Ireland. She gulped loudly as she took in every inch of him.

He must have sensed she was awake. "I'm sorry, I didn't mean to disturb you. I needed to wash myself and my clothes. I'll put a blanket around me until my clothes are dry."

Isla contemplated telling him she could dry his clothes with a touch of magic but decided she preferred his current state of undress instead.

He grabbed a sheet off the ground and wrapped himself in it. "I guess I need to go buy some clothes."

Isla snapped out of the haze she was in. It had been more than a year since she'd had sex and her body was making it very clear it was time to rectify that. She cleared her throat. "We can make our way back to the house if ye need to pick anything up. I dinna even know about ye being forced here with nothing."

He held up his phone. "This is all I need. Everything else is easily replaceable until we get back."

"Yer very easy-going aren't ye?"

He pursed his lips as he nodded. "It's a habit when you've been deployed as much as I have. As long as my family can reach me if need be then I'm at your disposal."

As much as she wanted to sit there admiring the view, the reality of their situation came back full force. She walked to the bathroom and grabbed his soaked clothing. Her eyes drifted closed as she focused on what she wanted to happen. With a few words in Gaelic, the items were clean and dry. She shrugged as she handed them to him.

He chuckled as he reached for them. "Well, magic does have its perks doesn't it." Their hands touched as he took the pile from her. "How long were you going to let me stay this way?"

Isla shrugged. "I didna want to use magic, I need to stay charged but I decided to take pity on ye. Perhaps tis time we pack and move on." For the sake of the Princess, she had to focus on her mission and not the beautiful man in front of her and the things she wanted him to do to her. They still had twenty-four days together. By the time it was over, she would likely be wound tight and desperate for a good shag.

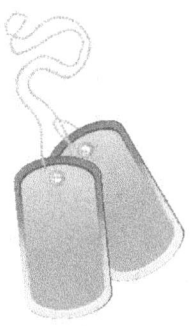

# Chapter Twelve

K illian held Ameria close as they walked down the sidewalk. If it wasn't enough that he was trying to come to terms with the supernatural creatures walking nearby, he also had to gauge if any of them posed a threat. A hairless creature with wrinkles covering every inch of its body stepped out of a coffee shop and almost bumped into him. It nodded at him in apology and went on its way. At least he had time to decide if he wanted her to continue spelling his necklace or if he wanted to forget all of it when the mission was done.

Isla pretended she hadn't even seen the man-sized slug thing as she continued walking. "We need to make our way to Dublin. The bigger the city, the harder it is fer the creatures to attack. There's a car rental up another block."

"And creating a vehicle for us would take up

too much energy."

She nodded. "Exactly, and I don't have time to study a book to learn how all the parts work. Besides, the more human we act, the less likely we are to draw attention. Large spikes of energy like the freak storms the bairn was creating caused people to take notice and come investigate. We need to avoid that at all costs."

Killian looked down at Ameria and stuck his tongue out at her. "Got it, keep her happy so we don't get killed."

Isla smiled at him as she opened the door to the rental agency. "Yer a quick study. Now, do ye mind taking cash and putting the car on your credit card? I need to stay off the grid and most places don't take cash anymore."

He shifted Ameria to his other arm and grabbed his wallet out of his back pocket. The older woman behind the counter waved them over. "Mornin', how can I help ye?"

Isla stood back and let him talk. "We need to rent a car one way to Dublin, and a car seat if you have one."

The woman reached out and stroked Ameria's cheek. "Of course, we can get ye all set up. We don't want anything to happen to yer beautiful family now do we?"

Killian heard Isla try to hide her chuckle behind him.

He handed Ameria off to her so he could fill out the paperwork. The baby only fussed a little, maybe she was finally getting used to Isla, or she understood what was at stake. Did infant elves understand more than infant humans?

The woman grabbed a car seat from a room off to the side then led them to a small black sedan parked behind the building. She walked him around the car then handed him the keys and left.

Isla stared at the car seat on the ground. "Do ye ken how to use these?"

Killian picked it up and put it in the backseat. "How hard can it be?"

Ten minutes later they were out of breath and Ameria was screaming. Apparently, elves don't travel in car seats, she was pissed they strapped her in and that was after spending a few minutes trying to figure out where all the belts went.

Isla handed Ameria a bottle and climbed out of the car. "That was a feckin' nightmare."

Killian twisted left to right, stretching his back. "Why would they make something so damn difficult? There have to be easier ways to secure a baby."

They looked at each other then burst into laughter. The absurdity of their situation was not lost on him.

He grabbed the keys out of his pocket and held them up. "It's your mission, do you want to drive?"

Isla shook her head. "Nay, I'd prefer to be ready to respond if anything happens."

He nodded and climbed into the driver seat. Isla buckled up then typed Waterford into the

GPS. "We'll stop here fer a night."

Brayan climbed out of the bag at her feet and curled up on Ameria's lap. Killian was relieved that the animal seemed to calm her as much as he did. He had been really afraid they were going to have to listen to her scream the whole way and possibly send lightning bolts down on them for ignoring her.

They had been driving for an hour when the peacefulness of the quiet ride was interrupted by Ameria fussing in the back seat.

Isla glanced back then turned around laughing. "Brayan says there is a bad smell coming from her. I think we need to pull over so I can change and feed her." She glanced around then pointed down the road. "There's a SuperMac up ahead, we can stop there."

Killian slowed down to move to the right lane. "That's like McDonald's, right?"

Isla shrugged. "Yes, but our chips are much better than yours."

"Chips are fries right?"

She smiled at him. "Exactly."

He turned the car into the parking lot. "While you're changing her, I'll get us some chips and soda. I need to decide for myself who has the superior french fry."

Isla grabbed the diaper bag and baby before

answering. "You're about to find out everything in life was a lie. There's very little food in America that is better than its counterpart in Europe."

Killian agreed with her first statement. Now that he knew paranormals were real, he did feel like his whole life had been a lie. It also left him with a lot of questions about their lack of helping with the world's problems but he'd have to save that for when they weren't running for their lives.

While Isla was in the bathroom, he grabbed their food and waited by the door. When she came out, she stole his breath away. He still couldn't believe he was spending every minute of the day with the woman he'd been fantasizing over for weeks. And she was way cooler than he'd expected.

She grabbed a chip from the container and popped it in her mouth. She chewed slowly while she watched him. "So, was I right?"

Killian hung his head in mock defeat. "I can't argue, your chips are better than our fries."

Isla stuffed more in her mouth as she smiled proudly at him. "I'd like to let her play fer a wee bit before putting her back in the car."

Killian glanced out at the barren trees. "It's freezing outside."

Isla sighed dramatically as she opened the door. "Ye haven't learned anything yet have ye?" She turned back and waved at him to follow. "Come on, it'll be grand."

He tossed the empty fry container in the garbage and followed the duo behind the restaurant. Isla kept going, straight into the woods. Once they were far enough not to see the building, Isla whispered something in Gaelic. Killian watched in awe as the area around them warmed considerably and the snow on the ground melted away. This explained how she was dressed so casually the day he saw her on her porch. She was her own personal heater. That trick would have come in handy more than a few times when he was deployed.

Isla carefully set Ameria on the ground and held her hands so she could stand. The baby was wobbly but determined. They watched as she tried taking a few tentative steps. Frustrated she wasn't making much progress, Ameria dropped to her butt then turned and crawled towards a dead bush that had been uncovered with the melting snow.

She touched a branch, and seconds later green leaves sprouted and began to grow. She giggled at her handiwork.

Killian stopped breathing; he couldn't believe what he was seeing.

Isla didn't appear fazed at all. "Elves are very in tune with nature. With her being royalty, she likely has many powers we don't know about yet." The crunching of snow was coming close. They turned and stared deeper into the woods. "Which could be bad because some beings can sense when magic is being done and track us."

Killian didn't hesitate. He grabbed Ameria and sprinted back to the car.

He didn't look back as he fought to get her strapped in her car seat. She had quickly figured out if she straightened her body, he wouldn't be able to buckle her.

Isla's nervous voice reached his ears. "Time's up, we need to go."

Killian stared down at Ameria. "We're trying to help you, please cooperate."

He doubted the infant understood, but she did sit back and let him finish strapping her in. With a heavy sigh, he closed the door and turned back towards the woods.

He had to blink to see if he was imagining the creatures or not. How would he describe them... they were a cross between a human and a hog. Thick hair covered most of their bodies but he could still see they were much bigger than them.

Isla pushed him to get in the car. "Those are mountain trolls. They won't hesitate to attack right here in public."

He got to the driver's side door and froze as he saw the creatures take off running toward them. A brick wall ten feet tall suddenly appeared. He glanced at Isla and saw her concentrating on the wall as she slowly got in the car. "Let's go, this will keep them until we get on the road."

Killian peeled out of the parking spot, glancing in the mirror expecting to see giant hairy creatures running after them. Part of him still wondered if this was all a part of some psychotic break and he was really locked away in a padded cell. He glanced at the woman next to him. He didn't want her to be a figment of his imagination. Even if it meant facing danger every day, he wanted to do it with her. He didn't care what came next, he would die protecting Isla and Ameria.

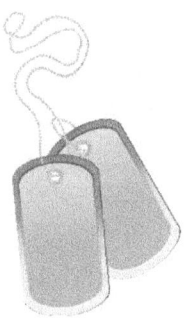

# Chapter Thirteen

K illian was thrilled when they pulled up to the hotel in Waterford. He hated being exposed in the car and would rather defend from their room.

Isla held the baby while he checked in. Ameria was finally getting more comfortable with her protector. He really did think the baby understood what was happening but how was that possible when she wasn't even a year old?

He touched Isla's back softly as he led them toward the elevator. "Let's get you guys in the room so you can do your warding while I go get food."

Isla glanced at Brayan on her shoulder. "That sounds like a plan. Brayan knows what to do."

The group made their way down the hall to the last room on the left. Brayan crawled down and took off to scout the hotel. Killian really wondered what the little guy did but if Isla trusted him,

Killian would too.

Once the girls were settled in, he went to the pub next door. It still shocked him to see random supernatural creatures sitting at the bar having a pint. He sat next to a tiny woman he assumed was a leprechaun.

The bartender walked up and set a small napkin in front of him. "What'll ye have?"

"Do you have a food menu. I'd like to order something to go."

The leprechaun glanced over and gave him a toothy smile. "An American, how exciting." She leaned forward and touched his arm. "I'll eat with ye if ye'd like company?"

Killian paused unsure what to say. "Sorry, my wife and daughter are back in our hotel room waiting for me to bring them food."

The woman pouted as she sighed heavily and turned back to nursing her Guinness. Killian grabbed the menu from the bartender. "Let me get a fish and chips and an order of chicken goujons." He had to admit even their names of foods were better than America's. Instead of chicken fingers, which he always thought sounded disgusting, they called them goujons. "I'm going to run next door and pick something up then I'll be back."

The bartender nodded and took the order to the kitchen. Killian smiled politely to the leprechaun as he turned and left. If he was lucky, everything would be ready when he got back so he didn't have to continue being ogled by the woman.

Killian crossed the street and went into the small market. With a quick scan, he found what he was looking for, bought it and a case of water then went back to get their food.

He stood next to the same barstool as before. He was glad it was less than a minute before a bag of to-go containers was brought out. He handed the bartender his card. "Put a round on my tab for the lady."

She sat straight and smiled at him. "I knew ye was a good one. Yer wife is very lucky."

Killian felt good as he made his way back to the hotel. He was glad he could do something nice for the woman.

He opened the door to their room and found Ameria asleep on the bed with Isla next to her rubbing her back. He wanted nothing more than to stomp across the room, scoop her off the bed and claim her as his.

She slowly climbed off the bed trying not to wake the baby. "What's this all about?"

Isla held up the tiny plant he had bought at the market.

Killian tried to look nonchalant. "Ameria likes plants. I thought she would like to have one."

The mage chuckled as she set the plant on the small desk in the corner. "I'm sure she'll love it. I'm putting you personally in charge of making sure we don't forget it anywhere."

Killian hadn't thought of that. Being on the run was work enough without making sure to drag a plant along, too.

He unpacked the food containers on the small table tucked against the far wall. "Chicken or Fish?"

Isla shrugged. "Why not split so we get a little of both."

He swapped a couple of the chicken tenders for one of the fish planks. "I grabbed some ketchup too if you want it for your chips."

Isla shook her head violently. "Seriously, that's the crap you put on your chips. Nay, I won't accept it." She dug through the bag and pulled out several small packets which she set down in front of him. "This is how you eat chips."

Killian picked up the condiment. "Malt Vinegar? That sounds disgusting." He tore open the corner of one. "It smells horrible too."

She snatched the packet from him and shook some onto a chip. "Try it."

He really didn't want to but she was so passionate about it he didn't want to disappoint her. Plus she could kill him with a flick of her wrist so better not to antagonize the mage.

The tip of his tongue brushed the side. "Ugh, so sour." She didn't move. Stealing himself he popped the chip in his mouth. *Yep, just as gross as I thought it would be.* "Yeah, it's not bad. I still like ketchup more though."

"Fine, more for me."

She doused the chips and the fish in the offending liquid. As she bit into the first chip she stared at him, as if daring him to say a word. Good to know Irish people take their vinegar very seriously.

The room was quiet while they finished eating, he didn't mind though. With all of the activity the last couple of days it was actually good for his PTSD to take a breather.

Isla wiped her fingers clean and sat back.

He could feel her studying him. "I can see the wheels turning in your head."

She tapped her finger against her mouth for a few seconds. "I'm wondering what yer story is. Why ye are in Ireland all alone?"

He sipped his water trying to decide how honest he wanted to be. The fact that she had revealed a whole world to him made it obvious he could open up to her. "I grew up an army brat, moving from base to base. When I turned eighteen, I immediately signed up to serve. It was never a question of whether I would join, it was expected of me. Over the last twelve years, I've done three tours of duty. I probably would have agreed to another tour if it weren't for the mortar attack five weeks before we were supposed to ship home." He reached into his shirt and held up the dog tag Isla had spelled. "Donovan was my best friend and I went home without him." He balled his fists against his mouth as he took a deep breath to control his emotions.

Isla wiped a tear from her cheek but stayed quiet.

He cleared his throat and started again. "As soon

as I was stateside, I visited his family and gave my condolences. Seeing other people grieve for him as much or more than I was overwhelmed me. I went home and told my parents I was retiring. As expected, my dad was pissed. He thought I was weak, especially when the PTSD attacks started. My mom was compassionate but never sided with me when my dad would lay into me."

Isla leaned forward and held her hand out. He stared at it for a second before reaching out and grabbing it. He watched her lips move as a ruin tattoo on her right arm burned bright for a second. Serenity flowed through him. For the first time in months, he didn't feel like he was suffocating. "Cale, one of the other mages, is an empath. He could almost permanently remove your pain, that was just a bandage."

Killian shook his head. "I wouldn't want him to. I earned this pain, I bled for it and I need to face it and get through it. That's how I came to be here. My mother's family was from Sligo, so I thought why not take a sabbatical somewhere I could be alone and work on myself."

Isla bit her lip. "And I dragged ye into another war. I am so sorry."

Killian looked over at Ameria sleeping peacefully on the bed. "You've given me a new purpose and one I know I can be good at. Whether it's good for me or not, I'm here to help you as long as you need it."

Killian didn't know what would happen after

their month with the baby was up. Would they go back to their own lives because the Princess had been what brought them together? Could he go back to America and have a normal, boring life after finding out about the supernatural world? Did he even want to?

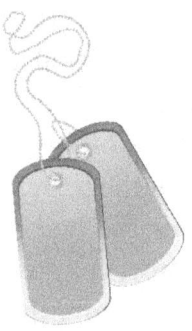

# Chapter Fourteen

**K**illian whistled as he walked down the hall carrying the pastries and coffee from a bakery down the road. He had bared his soul to Isla the day before and it didn't change the way she acted toward him. He felt no judgment from her for hiding away in Ireland. It felt good to spend time with someone who accepted him the way he was.

He tapped the room key against the door and pushed it open. He froze when he saw Isla's reflection in the mirror. She had quickly pulled her shirt on when she heard him coming in but it wasn't fast enough for him to miss the crisscrossing scars covering her back. Whoever had done that had been purposefully brutal. He decided right then he wouldn't ask her about it. She would open up when she was ready.

In a split second, the room broke out into chaos.

Ameria used the bed to balance as she walked over to the bedside table. She pulled on the lamp cord sending it toward the edge of the table. Isla dove across the bed, rolling off just in time to grab the lamp before it fell on the baby.

Isla rolled across the bed and picked Ameria up. "None of that now, yer gonna hurt yerself."

Ameria took a deep breath and let out a howl of anger. Killian set the food and drinks on the table and rushed over to help. It was too late though. The baby's emotions had crashed into them. They felt her anger and frustration. Killian was unaware that his hands had balled into fists and his jaw had tensed until it was almost painful.

As they were fighting the feelings that flooded them, Brayan ran to the corner where the plant was and used his mouth to drag it across the floor to Isla. As soon as he touched her, she was able to focus enough to look down. She grabbed the plant and handed it to Ameria. Like a gust of wind rushing through the room, the atmosphere changed drastically. Ameria let out a peal of laughter as she hugged the small pot against her chest.

Killian took a deep breath and sat on the edge of the bed. "Holy hell, that was intense. Now I understand why you were crying that day I came to your house."

Isla set Ameria on the ground with the plant and sat by him. "And it's just going to get stronger. This is probably why bairns don't usually get their powers until closer to puberty. Can ye imagine the destruction they could cause?"

They stared at the innocent-looking child then fell back against the bed laughing. After he caught his breath, he turned his face toward her. "I haven't been able to feel much of anything since Donovan died. Even though it wasn't great, it was nice to feel something again." That was the saddest part of the whole thing. He had been numb so long he welcomed anger and pain over the nothingness he'd been drifting in for months. Isla worried about dragging him into her war but didn't she realize she was saving him as much as he was helping her?

# Chapter Fifteen

I sla sat at the little table in their room and contemplated the leather-bound book in front of her.

Killian looked up from his seat on the floor by Ameria. "You've been staring at that for a while? Is it a really complicated spell book?"

Isla let out a heavy sigh. "I wish it were a book of spells. It's a memory book I started for the Princess. I don't know how much she's going to remember. I thought she'd like to have something to look back on her time with the Guild."

Killian climbed up in the chair next to her. "So, what's the problem?"

"There's no problem. I'm just trying to decide how honest to be. Do I write that she nearly flooded me home those first few days? Or how she hated me but fell in love with a perfect stranger on sight?"

Why she cared that the book is perfect was beyond her. The child likely wouldn't care about it either way. She pushed the book away and walked over to the window. She could make out the tops of trees behind the building across from them.

She loved the outdoors. The freedom of walking the hills around her home, of standing at the cliffs whenever she wanted. It had only been seven days and she was already antsy. Brayan must have felt her discontent and need for nature. He bounded into the room telling her about something he had found.

Isla excitedly turned to Killian. "Brayan says the hotel has a garden and sitting area on the roof. It's closed for the winter but we can easily work around that. How about we take our dinner up there?" She knew she sounded like she was begging but she really needed the fresh air.

Killian stood and grabbed his jacket off the chair. "I'll grab something from the restaurant down the street and meet you back here."

As the door closed behind him, Isla realized how much harder this would have been without him there. When she decided to go on the run, she didn't take into account the hundred little things that would come up like how to get food every day while hiding out.

Ameria's giggle had Isla looking at the child. "Killian really got himself into it with this one, didn't he?" The tiny plant he'd given the baby as a gift was now twice the size thanks to her Elven attention. If she kept at it, they'd be dragging around a six-foot tree and that wouldn't be inconspicuous in the least. "How about we go check out the roof?"

Isla picked up Ameria, grabbed the folded blanket off the shelf in the closet, and made her way to the door. "Come on Brayan, show us the way."

The tiny stout slipped under the door and chirped it was clear for her to come out. She followed him down the hall to the stairwell. They made it up two flights before getting to the locked door leading outside.

Isla whispered in Gaelic and smiled when she heard the click of the lock. As she swung the door open, she took a deep breath of the chilly air. Everything was better when she was outside. "Brayan this is perfect. What a great find."

The patio furniture spread around was covered for the winter. Isla pushed a table out of the way then sat Ameria on the ground while she shook the blanket out. "Let's let Uncle Killian know we're up here, shall we?"

She texted him a quick note to take the stairs then sat in the center of the blanket. Ameria crawled over and plopped in front of her, a tiny dribble of drool escaping down her chin as she smiled at Isla. "Does this mean ye are taking a liking to me now?" Not waiting for a response, Isla held her hand out and conjured a seed in her palm. "Let's see what you can do. Can you make this seed grow?"

Ameria studied the seed, her tiny finger stroked it gently. After a few seconds, the seed split and a tiny green sprout came from the center. They watched as it continued to grow until a blood-red rose laid fully bloomed in her hand. "Well now, that's a neat trick. I have no doubt yer going to be stronger than yer parents were."

Ten minutes and twelve flowers later, the door swung open and Killian walked out with bags in hand. "Brrrr, I thought you were going to warm it up."

Isla rolled her eyes then concentrated for a second. "There ye big baby." She glanced at Ameria as she whispered an incantation to make a bubble of warmth around them. "Humans are so wimpy aren't they?"

Killian handed her a bag of food before he sat down across from her. He pulled two cans of soda out of his jacket pocket. "I hope you like spaghetti."

Isla pulled the plastic lid off her tin container and took a deep breath. "There isna much I won't eat but this does smell grand."

"Let's hope it tastes as good." Killian shoved a large bite into his mouth. Isla couldn't resist laughing as he slurped the noodles and sauce splattered across his chin.

They fell into a comfortable silence as they ate. The only sounds coming from Brayan and Ameria who played like they were the bonded pair.

Isla set her empty container down and patted

her stomach. "Och, that was amazing."

Killian wiped his mouth with a napkin then leaned back against the couch behind him. "That was a good find. Have you had the real thing in Italy before?"

Isla nodded. "I lived in Venice for a few years but that was a lifetime ago."

Killian quirked an eyebrow. "When you say a lifetime ago... like your magic has let you live multiple lives?"

Isla chuckled. "Not exactly. I age very slowly so it feels like it's been a lifetime."

"I know you're not supposed to ask a woman how old she is but I think given the circumstances it's a reasonable question."

Isla watched his face closely; she was about to blow his mind. "Well, I was born in eighteen-ten so that makes me," she hadn't thought about it in a while, she had to pause to do the math. "Two hundred and eleven this year."

Killian's mouth opened and closed a few times, a range of emotions played out across his face. "I've been a good sport accepting everything you've shown me but I can't believe that."

"Tis the truth. Unfortunately, I was a young mage when the witch-hunting was at its worst here in Ireland. I was barely a teenager when my powers started manifesting. I was so excited to understand them I wasn't careful about who might see me. A neighbor saw me in the woods while I was learning how to create things from thin air. They turned me in and I was arrested." Without realizing she did it, Isla pulled her knees close to her chest and hugged herself. "For weeks they switched between starving me and beating me. They wanted me to give up the names of other witches. At some point, they realized I wasn't going to talk and scheduled my burning at the stake. They dragged me from my cell and displayed me in the center of town. They told the crowd if anyone else turned themselves in, I wouldn't be put to death. Of course, no one said a word. The priest ordered me whipped right there for all to see. I still remember the leather cutting into my skin. It's a feeling I don't think I'll ever forget."

Ameria must have been able to feel the intense emotions emanating from Isla. The babe crawled over to her and used Isla to pull herself up to standing. Ameria reached and touched her cheek gently. Isla could feel the warmth and love she was trying to give her. "Thank ye love."

Isla turned back to Killian who wasn't hiding the look of horror on his face from the telling of her tale. "They didn't stop until the crowd started screaming for them to end me suffering. They tied me to the stake as the priest droned on about the Devil inside me. His words gave me an idea. I used the last of me energy to create a bright light above the crowd with an angel coming down from the clouds. Everyone stood in silent fear as the being came down and wrapped me in a hug. Me creations can't speak so I had to get me point across the best way I could."

She paused. Even though it had been more than a century, the memory burned clear. "I created a hideous, horned creature and had it come up from the ground in front of the priest. It stalked closer and closer as the priest and his goons backed away in fear," she continued. "Me magic was almost gone. I was about to lose both creations when the priest threw himself to the ground and pleaded with what he assumed was Satan saying he would release me if it didna drag him to hell. He thought he had been doing God's work but was wrong. The rest of his men stood frozen in fear. He ran to the stake and untied me with shaking hands, apologizing over and over again. As soon as I was free, I fell to the ground and lost consciousness. The creations disappearing as soon as I closed me eyes."

Killian stared at her, likely searching for the right words. Isla didn't blame him; it was a fantastical story.

She took a long sip of water before continuing on. "I woke up three days later in me bed with me mum tending the wounds on me back. She told me the village was so outraged that the priest brought the devil to their doorstep that they ran him and his witch-hunting squad out. After that the town thought I was blessed by God. I couldn't go anywhere without being mobbed. Eventually, I left and traveled around Europe. I come back here every few decades and live in me family home. It's hard not being able to stay in one place for too long or people notice I don't age or die."

Killian rubbed his face as he let out a deep breath. "Suddenly everything I've experienced in my life seems so small and inconsequential."

Isla touched his arm. "Everyone's journey is different. Every day ye affect someone's life, don't ever take that for granted. I don't know if Ameria and I would be doing so well if it weren't for ye. Besides, I saw ye with yer shirt off. Ye have quite a few scars of yer own."

Killian shrugged. "Nothing as bad as being whipped but I did go through some hell." He cleared his throat and rolled to his knees, then picked up Ameria who had her arms up before he even reached for her. "Enough serious talk, I say we play with this one for a few more minutes then put her to bed." Ameria giggled as he tossed her in the air and caught her.

Isla's phone vibrated in her pocket. She pulled it out and saw an email from Lena.

Run the attached executable and your phone will be updated to the latest securities I've written. Let me know if you have any problems.

Isla tapped on the attachment and let the phone do its thing. She didn't really care to learn the details of the technology. As long as she could do the basics, she was good with that.

Once the phone was finished, she opened the Magecaster app and sent a group message.

Seven days down and still alive. We've had werewolves and trolls track us but we got away.

We're staying on the move, switching locations every couple of days. Ameria's powers are strong, ye guys will have yer hands full with her. I'll post another update in a few days.

-Isla & Ameria

She felt weird not mentioning Killian but she wasn't ready to tell them she brought a perfect stranger into the mission. For now, he was her little secret and she was going to enjoy it as long as she could.

Now to keep them alive for three more weeks, how much worse could it get?

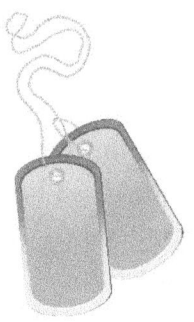

# Chapter Sixteen

**K**illian settled in behind the steering wheel and set his GPS toward Dublin. It was a new day, which meant another new city. Other than a couple of minor chases everything had been smooth. He would have thought protecting a hidden Princess a lot more dangerous.

After a few miles, the stretches of road got longer until there was no one around except sheep and cows staring at them as they drove by. *Could those be shifters too? Do I have to worry about every freaking animal we come across?*

Killian noticed the blue SUV speeding up on them first. It didn't take Isla long to notice it riding close. He tensed his hands on the steering wheel seconds before the SUV rammed into the back of their car. Ameria instantly started wailing then the SUV hit them again, sending them off the road. Killian stayed calm as they careened toward a large buildup of snow.

His head snapped back as they slid against a low fence that lay hidden under the snow. Isla's scream cleared his head as he watched her door open and she was pulled out of the car.

As Killian scrambled for his seatbelt, he heard the storm brewing above them. Ameria was not happy but she was going to have to hold on. His feet slid out from under him as he rushed to get around the car. He looked up just in time to see Isla create a sword nearly as long as she was. With sheer determination on her face, she swung it over her head hitting her attacker in the back. Her captor slumped to the ground, the snow around him turning red.

Isla threw the sword at him. "Protect the bairn."

His eyes bulged as she tossed the sword toward him. How did she expect him to catch it? At the last second, he reached out and managed to grab the handle without getting sliced. "Hey, I got it." He didn't have time to brag though. They were in the middle of a battle.

He stared at the weapon in his hand, he'd never actually held one before. "Couldn't she make me a gun? What am I going to do with this?" He muttered as he tried to get a feel for the weapon. Between the snow on the ground and the rain pouring down on them, it wasn't the ideal battleground but he would do what he must. Out of the corner of his eye, he saw another man bearing down on Isla. She created a second sword for herself and faced off against him. Killian could tell they were more than human but not what kind they were. It would have been really nice to know what he was dealing with ahead of time in case it had a weakness he could exploit.

Killian didn't have time to watch, a third man was stalking closer to him. Channeling his best Highlander impression, he raised the sword and pointed it toward the man. The blood drained from his face as he watched the man shift into a large bear, easily a foot taller than Killian. "Whoa big fella, that's cheating."

The bear roared in response. Killian swung the sword toward the animal, hoping to catch it off guard.

Killian was the one caught off guard as the weight of the sword threw him off balance. His feet slid on the snow as he tried to right himself. The bear saw its opening and swung its huge paw, tearing through Killian's shirt and ripping deep gashes into his ribs. The force of the hit was enough to throw him a few feet away. Burning pain tore through his side as he lay there trying to comprehend the fact that he just took a medieval sword to a bear fight.

The sound of Ameria's screams intensified as the car door was ripped open. The bear had shifted back to a man. Killian cradled his side as he got to his feet. With a quick glance toward Isla, she was deep in battle with another bear. He noticed the blood on her. Was it hers or the creatures? He grabbed his sword from the ground and ran at the man in the car. The sword slid easily through the man's spine. If it hadn't been for the ridiculous number of straps the car seat had, he would have been too late.

A loud grunt sounded behind him as he pulled the dead man from the backseat. "You're okay Ameria, we've got you." The words were mumbled from his lips as he fell to his knees. The blood loss was getting to him.

Isla ran to his side. "Where are ye hurt?"

Killian raised his arm showing the three large gashes across his abdomen. He growled as she laid her hands on top of the wounds. She whispered words over and over until he felt no more pain. He gasped when she pulled her hands away and the gashes had closed. "I can't completely heal you. It would take too much of me magic and I can't risk being completely drained."

Killian pulled himself up and tilted her chin to the side looking at a gash on her neck. "Can you at least close your own wound?"

She nodded as she covered the three-inch-long cut and whispered. Seconds later, it was still ragged but the blood flow had stopped.

Killian shook his head in awe. "We could have used you in battle. A lot of soldiers could have been saved."

Isla leaned in the car and pulled out Ameria to comfort her. The rain let up instantly. "It's a burden I've lived with me entire life. The Guild is impartial though, rarely is one side right when it comes to war so who are we to choose who to help? Our world's stability is delicate. We have no right to tip the balance of power one way or the other."

Killian knew she was right but it didn't make the idea of having the ability to save his friends but not doing it any easier.

Isla hugged Ameria close as the baby continued to whimper. "When these three don't return, the pack is going to come hunting. We need to get out of Ireland."

# Chapter Seventeen

I sla couldn't believe they had been attacked in full daylight where any human could have seen them. It was obvious the hunting parties wanted Ameria badly enough to break all rules the supernatural world held dear.

Killian held his finger up, stopping her before she got in the car. "One problem with getting out of Ireland, my passport is back at the cabin."

Isla leaned in and buckled Ameria in the seat before climbing back out. "Not to fret, I can create one fer ye."

She collapsed into the passenger seat and took a deep breath as she laid her head against the headrest. "I haven't had to expel that much physical and magical energy simultaneously in a while." The pit of her stomach where her magic was stored felt hollow. She was going to need to recharge. "I need to close me eyes fer a bit. Wake me if anything happens before we get to Dublin."

Killian nodded and closed her door.

It was the hundredth time she'd been grateful to him since they started their adventure. She knew she could rest and trust him to keep them safe.

Isla jerked awake when the car shut off. Killian smiled. "The rest of the ride was smooth sailing. Ameria slept the whole time too."

Isla ran her hands down her face, trying to shake the sleep from her brain. "I appreciate the escort. Now, where are we?"

Killian pointed out her window. "That hotel looks like it will do for the night but I'm not sure how we're getting in there looking like this." He waved at their tattered and bloody clothes.

Isla rolled her eyes. "Yer slow to learn sometimes aren't ye? I got this." She wasn't too worried about a quick glamour while they got to their rooms. She had more than enough magic restored for that. "Any preference on what ye'd like to be wearing?"

Killian shook his head. "I'm flexible."

Isla smiled devilishly. The man was too trusting. She whispered a few words and her clothes changed to a pair of jeans and a black sweater. Killian on the other hand said nothing, simply turned his head at her and quirked his eyebrow. "What? I think ye look dashing."

Killian sighed as he got out of the car in his khaki shorts, royal purple polo, and deck shoes. She doubted he had ever worn anything so basic before. He looked like he stepped out of a Ralph Lauren magazine. She'd been to America enough times to know most men didn't dress that way but it was still fun to mess with him.

He pulled Ameria from the car. The child clutched her plant in her arms. Isla led the way to the empty hotel lobby.

The young man behind the counter smiled politely at them. "Welcome to Dublin. Can I help ye?"

Isla leaned on the tall counter and smiled politely. "We'd like a room fer one night, please."

She waited patiently as he searched his computer. "I have a room on the third floor if that works for ye?"

Killian slid his credit card and ID across the counter.

Isla could already feel the strain of the constant glamour for both of them when she hadn't fully recharged yet. She sighed gratefully when they were given their room key after a short wait and made it upstairs.

She didn't mind the simple hotel room. She missed her cliffs and this was temporary. She walked around the room whispering the words to lock the wards in. Very few people on Earth could break her wards and now that Ameria wasn't driving her to distraction, she would sleep better knowing in their room at least, they were safe.

Satisfied with the protections she put in place, she dropped all magic. The clean clothes going with it. "I'll go buy ye some clothes. If ye have any trouble, Brayan will let me know."

Killian shook his head. "Absolutely not, you're being hunted. I will go."

Isla grabbed a clean sweater out of her bag and shook her head as she walked to the bathroom to change. "Yer clothes are a wreck. I can't glamour ye if yer not with me. It's fine, I promise."

As she closed the bathroom door and got a look at herself in the mirror, she couldn't help but groan. Dirt and mud were in her hair and on her skin. Her clothes were unsalvageable. She cracked the door open. "Ye didna tell me I look like a sluagh. I'll wash up then go."

Isla gave herself five minutes to sit under the hot water and not think or do anything. It had been more than a week since she'd taken any time for herself and given her only companion was a stout she was used to a significant more alone time.

With a sigh of resignation, she washed up and got out of the blessed stall. She said a quick word to dry her hair while she got dressed and then made her way out to the room. Her breath caught as she saw Killian sitting in a chair looking out the window as he held Ameria who was contentedly drinking her bottle. The man was gorgeous and good with kids to boot. She would be in trouble if she let her guard down for even a minute with him.

She was only good for a quick shag. She had no

interest in sleeping with someone she might come to care for only for them to grow old and die. No, she would never open herself up to that pain again.

Killian turned and smiled. "You look refreshed."

Isla sat on the bed and slipped on clean socks and her boots. "Aye, I needed that."

"So, question, what the hell is a sluagh?"

"Right, sorry about that. Easy explanation, they are spirits raised from the dead."

"You did not look like a zombie, I thought you looked beautiful like always."

Isla rolled her eyes at his attempt at charm. "Shite man, yer full of it. Now, I'll be off and will return soon."

Isla had a bounce in her step and a smile on her face. She'd had a peaceful shower, a quiet walk, and shopping all in one day.

Opening the door to their room, she stopped at the sight of Killian in a chair with a towel tied around his face. Ameria stood at his feet laughing up at him. "What's this now?"

She moved closer to hear the muffled words Killian mumbled. "Something died in her diaper. I tried changing her but the smell... it was just too much. I couldn't stop gagging, my eyes were watering. Maybe she pooped a sluagh? Do they smell like death?"

Isla shook her head at him as she picked up the

baby. "Are all men so dramatic? Come along Princess, we'll get you cleaned up."

Isla laid Ameria on the bed and undid her diaper. The putrid smell hit her nose instantly. "Ah Jaaaysus, ye weren't kiddin'."

Brayan had climbed on the bed but one sniff of the diaper had him scurrying away.

She whispered a couple of words and her nose was blocked long enough for her to get the job done.

Killian's jaw dropped. "Well that's just not fair, that's cheating."

Isla glanced over at him. "I'm happy to stand aside and let ye take over?"

He held his hands up. "No, no, I'm good right here."

Isla finished and set Ameria on the ground by her plant. "Yer clothes are over by the door if ye'd like to shower and change?"

"I can take a hint." He winked as he got up.

The bathroom door closed as Isla sat in the chair and let out a sigh. "We're getting there Princess, almost a third of the way over. Soon ye'll be with Nic in America and I'll be back in my cabin, alone like always."

Ameria stared up at her, drool running down her chin. The bairn was too cute for her own good.

Did she understand what was happening? Does she wonder where her parents were? Those questions plagued Isla but she knew there was nothing to do but keep her safe until she could be returned to her people.

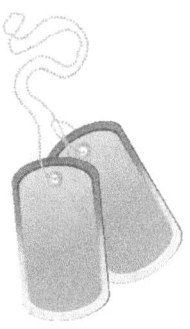

# Chapter Eighteen

K illian finished his eggs and toast and pushed the plastic container away. After the diaper debacle the previous day, nothing else had gone awry. They had played with Ameria until bedtime then watched a movie until they fell asleep.

Isla had offered again to share the bed or take turns but he had refused. The floor really wasn't that bad and this way he wouldn't risk making her uncomfortable. Other than sleeping separately, he was starting to feel like they were their own little family. He hadn't given much thought to marriage or kids but if he looked close enough, he would see the desire growing inside him with every passing day they were together.

Isla set down her teacup. "How are yer ribs today?"

Killian absently rubbed his side where he knew

the three long gashes were now tiny lines not giving away the truth of what had caused them. "Still sore but loads better than they were last night. I wanted to thank you for the sword, too. I'd never even touched one before so it was pretty cool to fight with one."

Isla smiled at him. "Ye looked like a fierce highlander from years ago. All that was missing was the kilt."

He pictured himself getting thrown to the ground, his kilt pushed up baring his ass to the world. "I don't know how they ever fought in battle wearing those."

She shrugged. "If it's all ye know, it doesn't bother ye at all."

"Good point. As awesome as that was though, do you think next time you can create a gun for me?"

Isla's eyes widened for a second. "I can't do it without reading up on it. I never bothered to learn how they work. I'll work on it fer ye."

Killian sipped of his coffee then scooped up Ameria who had crawled over to him. "The Nightshade Guild... what's that all about?"

Isla absently rubbed the ruin of the Guild on her wrist. "Thousands of years ago, the magical world was in disarray. Mages fought for power and didn't care who they cut down to get it. Humans were suffering right alongside the magical world. A group of mages banded together to try to bring order to the world. In a shockingly simple attack, someone poisoned the group with Nightshade.

None of the mages survived the attack but it was enough to shake the magical community. Mages from all over rose up and fought back against those trying to take control. They chose the strongest among them and asked them to watch over the community and police it fer the good of everyone. This new group called themselves The Nightshade Guild in honor of those they lost."

Killian shook his head. "Where there is power, there is greed."

Isla nodded her agreement. "The humans were in complete chaos. They had seen things they couldn't explain. The Guild worked tirelessly to remove any ideas humans had about the supernatural. Eventually, everything returned to normal. The leaders of the other groups were grateful to the Guild for stabilizing the world and allowing them to live peacefully unknown to the humans again." She made a bottle for Ameria and handed it to Killian. "Through the years, the rest of the supernatural community had started going to them fer help. After a while, it was clear that they had become an impartial group looking out fer everyone, not just mages, and they became the protectors and enforcers fer all kind."

Killian tried to process everything she had told him. "How did you come to join the Guild?"

Isla smiled; he could see his question brought forward good memories for her. "There are twelve mages. We're all experts in at least one type of magic. None are immortal but we do live an extraordinarily long time. However, Guild work is not easy. It can be dangerous and all-consuming. When a member chooses to leave the Guild, an incantation is spoken and the rune leaves that person with their memories intact and appears on the next most powerful mage of that magical type. It's up to the rest of the Guild to find that person and bring them into the fold." She held her wrist out and let him study the intricate symbol. "I was in Brazil, I lived there for a couple of decades with a few other mages. When the symbol appeared, it burned enough to wake me from a sound sleep. I knew of the Guild, everyone did. But I had never had any direct contact with any of them. I roamed fer a few weeks, sent messages to everyone in the magical community until finally one day Sunny and Demi found me and brought me to the Guild." Memories of those first days flooded her. She had been so overwhelmed by the others but they quickly showed her she was their equal. Not that she had a choice but it was the best thing to ever happen to her.

Killian sat back and blew out a deep breath. "It's all just so... fantastical. All I keep thinking is, *is this real life?*"

Isla felt for the man. Very few humans knew the truth of the world and it was always shocking at first. Rarely someone struggles so much with the knowledge the Guild is forced to intervene and wipe their memories. She didn't know him well but her gut told her he would accept this part of her. "I've been blessed with this ability and ask meself that question all the time."

Killian got up and tossed their trash in the can. "I guess we should hit the road?"

Isla checked the time on her phone. "Aye, the ferry to Holyhead, England leaves in a couple of hours."

She hoped leaving Ireland would give them a little peace. All of the hunting parties that had found them so far were low-level goons. As long as it stayed that way, the rest of the month wouldn't be so bad.

# Chapter Nineteen

K illian scanned the dock as they walked off the ferry. Being trapped on a boat with nowhere to run if someone did attack had kept him tense for the last couple of hours. He was a good soldier though, it was ingrained in him and he wouldn't let them down.

Isla checked her phone. "There's an Inn a couple of blocks over. Let's get a room fer the night then we'll get another car in the morning."

He scrunched his eyebrows together. "You heard them when we returned the last car so damaged. They told us not to come back. Ever."

Isla waved her hand dismissing his concern. "That's already been taken care of. I messaged Lena and she's already hacked their system and erased ye."

Killian didn't like the sound of being erased so easily by a powerful mage but it was exactly what they needed if they were going to keep moving.

The smell of garlic reached his nose, and his mouth instantly watered. The closer they walked to the hotel, the stronger the smell got. Until the scent led them to a small restaurant next to their destination. Killian's stomach growled. "Would you mind if we ate inside? Not that floor picnics in our room aren't great but I'd love to eat somewhere the plates and silverware aren't plastic."

Isla chewed her bottom lip as she glanced up and down the road. "I suppose me magic's recharged enough in case something happens." She waved her hand toward the door.

Killian gave her a dazzling smile. He hadn't actually expected her to agree. He held the door and let her walk inside first. The interior was as quaint and tiny as the outside implied. A waitress looked up from the table she was getting an order from and smiled. "Sit where ye'd like, I'll be with ye soon."

Isla groaned as she pulled the bags off her shoulders and sat. "Having a bag with infinite space does add some weight."

Killian sat and turned Ameria so she was on his lap facing the table. "You should have said something. I can take it for you, or at least take turns."

Isla held her hands up. "Ye have yer hands full with the bairn. I can handle a couple of backpacks."

"Afternoon lovelies, would you like a cuppa or a pint?" The older woman with gray curls and a warm smile handed them each a menu.

Killian had no idea what a cuppa was and felt stupid asking. "Pint for me please." He had learned after a couple of weeks that a pint was Guinness.

Isla scanned the menu. "I'll have a cuppa please."

That was a relief, at least he'd learn what it was without admitting ignorance.

"Anything for yer daughter?"

Killian and Isla met each other's gaze. Did she feel the same sense of excitement each time someone thought they were a family? "No thank you, she's still drinking formula."

The waitress walked away and left them in silence. Why did he feel awkward?

Isla set down her menu and leaned back in the chair. Killian had already figured out what he was ordering but he continued to study the menu as if it had more than one page.

When he didn't think he could stall any longer, the waitress returned with his pint and a cup of hot tea. Now cuppa made sense but how did they expect visitors to know?

"Are ye ready to order?"

Isla handed the woman her menu. "I'll have the fish pie."

Killian scrunched his nose. He liked seafood as much as the next person but that just sounded gross. "I'll have the brisket bap." He hadn't had barbeque in months. Just thinking about the pulled beef that was coming made his stomach growl.

Ameria reached up and rubbed the scruff on his chin, her giggle making others in the restaurant turn and smile at her.

Isla cocked her head to the side, studying them. "How are ye so good with wee ones?"

Killian shrugged. "Ameria is the first baby I've ever held. I don't think it's that I'm good with kids, I think I lucked out the Princess liked me." He pretended to bite Ameria's hand making the child giggle louder. "What about you? Other than her Highness here, have you been around many kids?"

"Ye don't live as long as I have and not run into a kid or two but I've never gotten close to any."

The loneliness in her tone was evident. "Do you want kids of your own?"

She pursed her lips before answering. "Besides the other mages, everyone around me dies. Why would I bring a child into the world and only get to spend seventy or eighty years with them? Can you imagine trying to go on living after that?"

In his mind, he pictured Isla as young and beautiful as she was right then sitting beside an elderly woman and saying goodbye to her. That was a fate worse than death. "I just assumed your children would be mages. I'm sorry."

She shook her head sadly. "There's no rhyme or reason to who is born with magical abilities and who isn't. I've not found anyone else in me family who's a mage so there's no guarantee me child would be."

The waitress returned humming as she set

their plates down. She was blissfully unaware of the heavy topic she had walked up on.

They ate in silence until Isla let out a deep breath. "It's not like I've been alone all this time. I have fallen in love before but he didn't want to live as long as I did. He felt life lost some of its sparkle by not having a limited time to experience it."

Killian took his time dissecting her words while he ate the best barbeque he'd ever had. "This is way more complicated than I imagined." He hated the idea of her having to say goodbye to anyone she got close to.

Isla reached across and grabbed his hand. "Don't feel sorry fer me. I have thought about what it would be like to have a family. If I met the right man and he wanted to share me whole life, I'd not rest until I'd found the magic needed to do that. If we were to have children and they didn't have me magic, I'd let them grow up and make that decision on their own. If they chose a normal human life, it would devastate me but I would accept their choice."

Killian swallowed past the lump in his throat. "All magic comes with a price."

Isla nodded. "Exactly. I go on living as a mage of the Guild at the expense of not having a family. I've made peace with me decision."

Killian couldn't hold back the laugh that suddenly built up inside him.

Isla's eyebrows scrunched together. "What's so funny?"

"I was thinking about how I believe in Aliens, always have and yet I find all of this so unbelievable."

"Yer telling me, ye believe in little green men but not in witches?" Isla laughed until her side hurt.

Killian squinted his eyes at her. "Oh sure, mock the human." Ameria squirmed in his arms, yawning as she rubbed her eyes. "I think it's time we get a room and let this one take a nap."

Killian had a lot to think about. If his feelings for her did intensify he'd have a decision to make and he wasn't sure if living for hundreds of years really was as exciting as it sounded. Four months ago, he'd been contemplating if he wanted to live another day and now, he's was pondering the idea of living for centuries. One thing was for sure, his trip to Ireland was definitely having an impact on him.

# Chapter Twenty

Y ou don't really know a person until you're on the run with them, trying to stay alive. With each passing day, Isla grew more attached to Killian and his easy-going manner. For the last two days, they had zigzagged around England. He enjoyed the views and asked questions about each place they visited. They had started in Manchester then went over to York, down to Nottingham, over to Gloucester, and stopped for the night in Bath. She wished they could have stayed a night in each place so he could see everything but they had to keep moving and get somewhere safe.

Ameria had fussed when they put her back in the car this morning. Brayan saved them from a miserable drive through Southampton into London by keeping her entertained as he rolled onto his back and let her pet his belly.

Killian craned his neck toward the window to get a better view of the massive stone towers of the Tower Bridge. "If I haven't said it before, thank you for taking me on this adventure. I probably wouldn't have snapped out of my funk and explored these other countries if it weren't for you."

"It's nice being with someone who appreciates all of this. I've seen these sights so many times, I forget how beautiful they are."

Once they were off the bridge, Killian sat back. "Are there any sights in the world you haven't seen?"

"Oh, sure. I've not been to America or Canada." It took her a second to remember everything she had done over the last two hundred years. "I haven't been to Australia or New Zealand yet either."

"How have you not been to America?"

Isla quirked an eyebrow at him. "Eh, everyone brags about how amazing it is, I guess I just never bothered to find out fer myself." She paused as the GPS spoke the next direction. "I wasn't trying to be spiteful or anything, just haven't gotten around to it yet."

He looked over and shook his head at her. "Well, when this is all over, I formally invite you to visit America and let me take you around to see some sites."

Heat rushed Isla's cheeks. Should she read more into his invite? If he was thinking about seeing her after this insane assignment maybe he was interested in her?

The GPS beeped after a few more turns. Killian circled around until he found a parking spot on the road. "You're sure your friend isn't going to mind me being here?"

Isla stretched as she got out of the car. "Trust me, Kleolise would never turn away a man. You'll understand why when you meet her." She knew she was being cryptic but she really wanted to see how he responded to meeting a Siren.

He followed behind with Ameria as they made the short walk to the other woman's house. "This is a nice place."

Isla scanned the small house Kleolise took such good care of. "I guess she does, again, I forget to notice these things anymore." When had she stopped appreciating the beauty of the world?

The door swung open as Isla raised her hand to knock. The curvaceous redhead threw herself at Isla and squeezed her tight. "It's been so long. You don't visit often enough."

Brayan squealed as he popped out of the backpack and leaped at Kleolise. "Of course, you're the real reason I want to see her. Come here cutie."

Isla chuckled as she stepped aside and pointed at Killian and Ameria. "And this is the reason we are here now."

Kleolise reached out and grabbed Killian's arm. "Come inside, don't be shy. I want to see the world's most wanted Princess."

"Thank you, ma'am, for letting us stay here."

She clucked her tongue. "Call me Kleo or don't call me at all." She winked at him as she led them down the hall toward the sitting room. "You are a handsome one aren't you." She glanced past him and looked at Isla. "Did you know the baby came with a big strapping man, too?"

Isla rolled her eyes at her friend. "Don't mind her Killian, she has no filter."

Kleo pointed at the couch. "Make yourselves comfortable, I'll grab us a cuppa."

As soon as she turned the corner, Killian leaned close. "You're sure we can trust her? She seemed really interested in Ameria."

Isla grabbed the baby and sat her in the middle of the floor. "I saved her life many years ago and she's sworn complete loyalty to me since. I trust her with me life and the life of the bairn." She could see he wasn't convinced. "I appreciate yer concern, while we are safe here, I don't think we should let our guard down for even a minute. I trust ye to help keep us safe."

Kleo strolled in carrying a tray. Isla watched as the other woman handed Killian a cup, her hand stroking his as she did. Isla knew what her friend was doing, she didn't lure men to their deaths any longer but that didn't stop her from trying out her powers once in a while to see if they still worked.

Killian set the cup on the side table. "It's been a long drive. Can I use the bathroom?"

Kleo pointed down the hallway. "Second door on your left."

As soon as the door clicked shut, Kleo pounced on Isla. "Oh my god, he is gorgeous. How are you living with him and managing to keep your hands to yourself?"

Isla chuckled at her friend's enthusiasm. "Under different circumstances maybe there could be more but right now all of our attention needs to be on that wee one." She pointed at Ameria who was crawling around, chasing Brayan. "Before this happened, I had been keeping an eye on him, thinking about a fling with him but then..." She let the sentence trail off. No need to bring up the murder of the King and Queen again.

Kleo leaned close. "I don't think you understand. I threw everything I had at him and none of it affected him at all. You know what this means right?"

Isla had no idea what it meant.

"When a man resists a siren it's because they've met their one true mate."

She couldn't really be implying Isla was his mate, could she? He may have met his mate but that didn't mean it was her. He could have met the woman back in America. Isla's hands grew sweaty trying to comprehend what her friend was telling her. In the end, she knew the real reason she was deflecting was that she didn't want a human as a mate. Didn't want to worry about the lifespans of her family.

Kleo cleared her throat and spun around as Killian came back into the room. "You two certainly have the whole paranormal community in a tizzy. It's been almost two weeks. Word has pretty much spread everywhere. Some are putting it together that only the Guild would be powerful enough to hide the Princess."

Isla groaned. That was the last thing she wanted to hear. "I guess that means the attacks on us are going to ramp up."

"Don't expect the Elves to help either, the Kingdom is in turmoil with everyone pointing fingers at each other. Whoever did this created quite a mess."

Killian sat on the floor and smiled at Ameria as she crawled to him. "You don't murder royals just to cause chaos."

Isla plopped down on the couch and let out a heavy sigh. "It's not about chaos. The assassin would have wanted to keep this secret as well until they got their hands on Ameria. Ye see all Elven magic is controlled by the one who wears the crown. That person could turn the tap on or off and plunge the whole Elven community into magical darkness. Me guess is the assassin wants to get control of the crown."

Kleo squeezed her friend's hand. "Why don't you go and stay with Morwen in Scotland. Two mages have to be better than one?"

"I'd love to but the Elven council made us promise only one of us would be with the Princess at a time. They were worried about us getting complacent, or the baby getting attached."

Kleo set her teacup down and let out a sigh. "Well, at least you have a handsome man with you. You guys look like a beautiful, young, family. People won't be expecting that."

The object of their attention crawled into Killian's lap, yawned, and started to fuss.

He pointed at the diaper bag. "Can you toss me a diaper so we can get her cleaned up?" Isla dug in the bag and tossed him wipes and a diaper. When he was done, he picked her up and curled her against his chest. "I think we need to get this one to bed."

Out of the corner of her eye, Isla noticed Kleo fan herself. She understood exactly what the other woman was thinking. *What a man.* The siren cleared her throat and stood up. "Follow me." She took them upstairs and opened the first door on the left. "It's not much but it's all I have."

Isla pursed her lips together trying not to laugh. It was by far the tiniest room they'd been in. The bed couldn't have been bigger than a full and any space they may have had was taken up by a playpen. There would be no way for Killian to sleep on the floor.

Killian cleared his throat. "I can sleep on the couch downstairs."

Kleo shook her head. "That old thing is lumpy as hell and way too small for you. I'm sure the two of you can share a bed without issue, right?"

Isla rolled her eyes at her friend's obvious attempt to push them together. She stepped inside and set her bags on the bed. "I'm okay with it if ye are?" Butterflies danced in her stomach waiting to hear his response.

Killian slowly bent over and laid the now sleeping Princess in the playpen. "I don't know. Can I trust you to be a lady? I don't want you taking advantage of me."

Isla's mouth opened and closed. She had no words.

Kleo snorted. "I'll bring you some towels, the bathrooms across the hall." She started to close the door behind them then paused. "Just remember these old walls are very thin." She winked before turning and leaving them alone.

Killian rubbed the back of his neck. "She is quite the unique woman, isn't she?"

Isla's eyes rounded as she shook her head. "Ye have no idea. She's the one to take to a pub if ye want to have such a good time ye can't remember it the next day."

Unfortunately, that had happened more than once but Isla could never say no to her friend's bubbly personality. Isla tended to be more serious than she should be so she depended on Kleo to help her loosen up once in a while.

Killian chuckled as he dug through his backpack. "I can't say I've ever had that experience." He pulled out the T-shirt and shorts he slept in. "I'm going to get changed. I really don't mind sleeping on the floor or the couch. Think about it and let me know when I come back."

Isla nodded and watched him walk out the door.

Using the time to herself, she changed into the tank top and shorts she'd brought and climbed into bed. "It is tiny isn't it?" She mumbled. If she stretched her arm out, she reached the other side. Killian was huge. They were about to get very comfortable with each other.

The door swung open silently. Killian quirked an eyebrow at her in bed. "Someone's a bed hog."

Isla scoffed as she sat up. "I am not! I'm on the edge of me side, I can't give ye any more room if I tried."

He smiled broadly at her. "I'm just teasing you." He set his clothes on top of his bag. "Do you realize how much thicker your accent gets when you're angry or stressed?"

She hadn't noticed that but now that he mentioned it, she would forever notice it.

Her body tensed as the mattress shifted under his weight. He was close enough she felt the heat radiating off him. How did men always seem to stay warmer than women?

She gently laid her arm down by her side. Electricity shot between them as their arms touched. He didn't move away. The tension was too much. "Ye must be used to sleeping in strange places aren't ye?"

Killian's head swished across the pillow as he turned to look at her. "Are you implying I sleep at strange women's houses often?"

Isla gasped. "Nay, I meant when you were in the service."

Killian chuckled. "I know what you meant."

She shoved her elbow into him. "Yer a right git aren't ye."

"I aim to please."

Isla snorted. "Is that how ye woo women in America?"

Goosebumps ran down her arm as she heard his breathing speed up. She could feel his eyes on her. "Is that what you want, me to woo you?"

That's exactly what her body wanted but her mind was screaming for her to keep him at a distance. "Don't flatter yerself, just because ye have muscles for days and gorgeous eyes doesn't mean yer charm's going to work on me."

Her eyes fluttered closed. Had she really said that?

Her mouth went dry as she felt him rub his fingers gently against her hand. She turned her hand palm up, waiting to see what he would do.

The faintest stroke went across her open hand. His fingers gently slid between hers. The room was silent except for their intermingled breathing. Such an innocent touch shouldn't excite her, but it did. It excited her from her head to her toes. She pictured herself rolling over and straddling his hips.

A frustrated growl escaped as she unlocked hands and rolled away. She didn't want a human mate no matter what her body was telling her. Two more weeks, that's all she had to do, keep her legs closed and her heart safe until their mission was over and he was back in America.

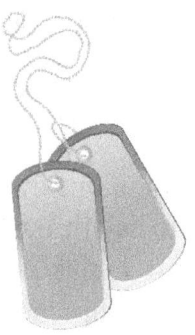

# Chapter Twenty-One

The smell of bacon frying broke through the intense sex dream he'd been having about Isla. Two more minutes and it would have been pure mental bliss.

He leaned over Isla and smiled at Ameria. She stood in the playpen jumping up and down excitedly. "Someone's chipper this morning." He whispered as he tip-toed over to her. "Should we go get some breakfast and let Isla sleep?"

A loud yawn behind him had him turning. "It's okay, I'm up and I agree we need to go eat whatever it is that smells so good."

Killian lifted the Princess up and let her curl against him. "I'll change her while you make a bottle?"

Out of the corner of his eye, he saw Isla stretch. Was she still upset about the night before? Had he been reading her signals all wrong?

She dug through her bag and pulled out clothes. "Bottle, shower, then food. I want to stand for a ridiculously long time under a shower with water pressure."

Killian's laugh came out forced and awkward. Why did she have to say things like that? Did she not understand how men's brains worked? The image of her naked had him holding back a groan.

He finished closing the new diaper as Isla walked close and leaned over Ameria. "Good morning, your Highness. Your breakfast is served." She stood back up, her hands on her hips. "It must be nice to be waited on hand and foot, food brought to ye in bed."

Nerves filled Killian. He didn't know what to say. He felt like he needed to apologize for making her uncomfortable the night before. Her head tilted to the side. "Are ye okay?" A gentle knock at the door broke the tension. "I'll get that."

Kleo stood on the other side smiling brightly. "Good morning. Breakfast is almost ready. If you want, I'll take the Princess downstairs while you two get cleaned up?"

Isla turned and gave him a questioning look. "It might be nice to not have to rush right?"

He still wasn't sure the woman could be trusted but if Isla thought it was safe then he would cautiously give her friend the benefit of the doubt. "Sure, sounds good."

Isla stepped back and let him hand America off to Kleo.

He closed the door and leaned against it. "What

kind of supernatural is she?"

Isla grabbed her clothes from her bag. "A siren, like the kind who seduced men and lured them to their deaths."

He shuddered. "Well that sounds horrible."

Isla patted his shoulder consolingly then opened the bedroom door, making him get off it. "I'll save ye some hot water."

As soon as the door closed behind them, he flopped onto the bed. "Get a hold of yourself, you're here to do a job." He reprimanded himself then hopped up to make the bed. Thanks to Bootcamp it was ingrained in him not to leave a mess before he left a room.

He stood at the window looking out over the rows of houses. He tried to imagine settling down in one with his wife and kids. Was he ready for that or was he still too broken?

Isla walked in with a towel wrapped around her head. "All yers."

He nodded as he grabbed his clothes and passed her. He hoped the walls weren't too thin. He was going to need to relieve some pressure while he was in there or he'd never survive two more weeks with her.

Killian looked at the pictures on the walls as he made his way to the kitchen. It looked as though she had kids and grandkids but she didn't look old enough for that. Did Sirens age as slowly as Mages? He shook his head. A siren, he was staying with a freaking siren. This trip kept getting weirder and weirder.

Laughter rang down the hall as he followed it to find the women sitting around a small table. "What's this?"

Isla turned and gave him an exasperated look. "Did ye know the wee one can eat food, too? No one told me, I thought it was formula only for her." The plate in front of Ameria had scrambled eggs and banana slices on it.

Kleo shook her head. "I'm kind of surprised she's still alive considering you two apparently don't know anything about kids."

Isla snorted at her friend. "Why don't they send a manual with these things? The Elves just expected us to know?"

Killian took a bite of the banana slice Ameria was holding up to him. "You're not a thing, are you?"

Isla rolled her eyes. "Ye know what I mean."

Kleo grabbed a cup and filled it with coffee. "There's plenty, take whatever you'd like."

The spread of food was the best thing he'd seen in two weeks. It was a feast compared to their to-go containers.

Ameria continued to feed Isla as Killian finished his food. "I think you're eating more than she is."

Isla nodded. "Aye, but she likes me now and I'll take that."

He got up and washed his plate. Through the tiny window above the sink, the sun reflected off of a building. "Kleo, what's that back there."

She got up and looked where he was pointing. "That's my greenhouse. I love plants but not many love the English winters. This way I can have blooms whenever I want."

An idea formed. "I think I know exactly where Ameria would like to spend the day."

Isla clapped her hands in front of the baby. "Do ye want to go see some flowers?" Ameria giggled and raised her arms to be picked up. "Leave the dishes and I'll clean up in a bit."

Kleo waved her off. "You're my guests, go have some fun and let me take care of this."

Killian held the back door open. "Shall we?"

The trio stepped through the dewy grass to the glass building in the back corner of the yard. Warm, dry air hit them as they stepped inside. It felt like a tropical island, not England in January.

Ameria caught sight of the blooms and wiggled excitedly in Isla's arms. As they walked deeper down the aisles of flowers, the vines and leaves leaned toward them, as if drawn to them, or more likely the Princess.

Ameria held her hand out toward an orchid, Isla stepped closer and gasped as the flower wrapped itself around the baby's arm.

Killian shook his head. "You weren't kidding about Elves and nature."

Isla squinted her eyes. "Let's see how strong

she is." She glanced around then walked toward a table in the corner. "Okay little one, let's put ye down." Killian moved a set of gloves off the table so Isla could sit Ameria in the center.

The smell of fresh dirt reached his nose as Isla opened a bag of soil and filled a small pot that was stacked under the table. She rifled through various containers of seeds then picked a few out. "Can ye make this grow?" She set the pot in front of Ameria and stepped back.

They stood in stunned silence as the Princess leaned forward and pushed her fingers into the soil. Seconds later, multiple sprigs of green popped up. The room was silent as they watched the stems grow, the leaves unfurled, and several flowers opened. Within a minute, she had a fully grown bush taller than her.

Ameria sat back and giggled. Drool ran down her chin as she smiled at them. She bounced up and down, clapping as she looked behind them.

Killian was almost afraid to turn around. Laughter bubbled up as he saw all the flowers that were within a few feet of them had grown considerably since they had walked past them.

They turned back, eyes wide staring at Ameria.

Isla covered her mouth as she studied the Princess. "Shite, I've never seen an Elf this powerful at this age. Most don't even start showing bits of magic until they hit puberty. This one is going to be stronger than her parents, I can feel it."

Killian didn't know what to say to that. He was

way out of his depth.

Isla turned back to the packets of seeds. "Let's see what else she can do."

A whistle behind them had everyone's attention turning. Kleo touched a few of the flowers that had grown. "That's a neat trick, isn't it? I could have used her help when I was first learning to grow these."

Isla picked Ameria up and set her on her hip. "She's got the power to turn the whole Elven world upside down. Best not make an enemy of this one."

Kleo nodded enthusiastically. "That's for sure. Now, come on, lunch is ready."

Killian squinted his eyes. "Didn't we just eat?"

Kleo held her phone up. "Yes, three hours ago."

"I didn't realize we were in here so long."

Kleo picked up a pot off the floor. "It looks like I'll need to make a run for more supplies."

They glanced around and realized they had filled several pots with full-grown blooms and Ameria had helped out the rest of the partially grown ones around the building.

Ameria yawned loudly as she played with a vine that was wrapping itself around her leg.

Isla pulled the climber off her. "I think ye need a nap. We pushed ye too hard."

As soon as they stepped out the door Ameria

let out a scream and flailed in Isla's arms.

Killian glanced up. "Oh no." The crash of thunder and freezing cold rain poured down on them. The group took off, running toward the house.

He pulled the door open and let the others go in first.

Isla rushed over to the table and grabbed the small pot of flowers from the center. "Look, there's more in here fer ye to play with."

Ameria sniffled as she hugged the pot close. The rain quieted then stopped. Isla let out a deep breath. "I hope ye don't mind but she's going to nap with this."

Kleo held her hands up. "She can keep them. I don't want to experience that tantrum again. You guys really have your hands full."

Isla snorted as she laughed. "Nay, the other mages do. They thought they were so smart not taking the first shift. They didn't think about how much stronger she was going to get each month. If this goes on for months, I hate to see how the others are going to handle her."

Killian tried to imagine a slightly older Ameria running through the woods, the trees, and leaves helping hide her from whatever mage was supposed to be in charge. The poor souls had no idea what they were in for.

# Chapter Twenty-Two

I sla sat at the kitchen table, the blank pages of America's memory journal taunting her.

The creaking of the backdoor made her jump. "Here let me help." Isla created two extra arms and took the grocery bags from Kleo.

"Um, that's different."

Of course, Killian would choose that moment to come into the kitchen with Ameria. Isla couldn't turn around. She didn't want to see his face. Was he disgusted?

Kleo snickered at them. "I bet you're imagining what that would be like in the bedroom." A fifth arm shot out and smacked her friend. "Just a joke, sheesh."

Isla's face felt like it was on fire.

Killian cleared his throat. "Is there anything I can help with?"

She let out a deep breath, grateful he wasn't

making a big deal out of it.

Kleo shook her head. "As you can see, we have it *handled*."

Isla was going to kill her friend when they were alone again.

The siren finished putting the milk away then sat at the table. "I should tell you what's going on out in the real world. The magical community has been whispering that patrols of vampires and shifters have been increasing in the area."

Isla let out a deep breath. "I'm not surprised. We've been here for four days now. This is the longest we've stayed anywhere. They must be picking up our tracks."

Killian handed Ameria to Isla while he made a bottle. "So, where do we go from here?"

Isla peaked up at him. "How do you feel about the Chunnel?"

He handed the bottle to the Princess and sat. "You mean get closed into a metal tube and shot under the ocean at a high rate of speed?"

"Yep, that's the one." Kleo was too happy to confirm that for him.

Isla rested her hand on his. After four days of sleeping in close quarters, they had gotten more comfortable with small touches. The sexual tension was still running high though so they kept it to a minimum. "I'm a mage remember? I won't let anything happen to ye while we're hurtling underwater."

Killian crossed his arms over his chest. "That's

not helping."

Isla bent close to Ameria's head. "Uncle Killian is just a big baby. Don't let that soldier persona fool ye."

Kleo stroked Ameria's cheek. "I'm going to miss you guys but I know you have to go. Let me make lunch first."

It had been a very long three-hour ride in the Chunnel. Isla's hand hurt from Killian squeezing it so many times. The man was fearless in battle, not afraid of being shot but one little train did him in.

The speaker overhead announced they'd reached their destination. "Welkom in Belgie. Bienvenue en Belgique. Willkommen in Belgien. Welcome to Belgium."

Killian walked close to Isla's side, the baby tucked tightly against her chest. "Why'd they say it so many times?"

"Belgium has three official languages, Dutch, French, and German. They are welcoming everyone, even Americans." She winked at him. It was bizarre to her that he only knew one language. Sure, she'd been alive a couple of hundred years and spoke twenty languages fluently but he could have at least tried to learn one other one.

Killian held the door to the station open for Isla. "Have you come here often?"

She shook her head. "I passed through once but never stayed. I'm excited to try their chocolate."

"Aren't they supposed to have really good waffles, too?"

Isla scrolled through the map app on her phone. "Aye, waffles, and beer." She glanced down the road. "There's a car rental up ahead."

"We're not staying here?"

She shook her head as they pushed through the crowd. "Nay, we have a three-hour ride into Brussels. We need to stay in highly populated areas we can blend in."

Not to mention she'd always wanted to stay near the canals so why not get a little pleasure while risking their lives?

Isla was relieved the drive had been uneventful. If anyone knew they were there, they weren't making themselves known yet.

The GPS beeped the last direction as Killian pulled into the hotel she had reserved on her phone.

Killian whistled as he glanced up and down the road. "This is so much better than I was picturing."

Isla couldn't hide the eagerness in her voice. "I know! Now that we're here, I realize how excited I am."

They made their way to the lobby and waited their turn to check-in.

The older gentleman behind the counter

waved them forward. "Welcome, how can I help you?"

Isla held her phone out with the confirmation email. "Reservation for Stewart."

"Of course, we have you on the fourth floor overlooking the canal. Would you like a portable crib sent up?"

Isla wasn't sure how to answer. Would Killian go back to sleeping on the floor while she shared the bed with Ameria? She wasn't ready to give up the comfort of sleeping next to him. She turned and looked at him.

Killian searched her eyes. She gave him a tiny smile. He nodded before answering the concierge. "A crib would be wonderful."

"Of course, sir. It will be right up. The elevator is to your right. It's small but you might all fit in one trip."

They were used to that. They'd been lucky all of their hotels had had an elevator, many didn't. She had used her magic more than once to get them up or down quickly, partly in fear of the tiny, ancient death traps malfunctioning.

Brayan hopped out of Isla's bag as soon as they were off the elevator. The animal knew what to do. If there was a supernatural being in the hotel, he'd sniff them out immediately.

They were the third room on the left. She bounced on her toes waiting for Killian to open the door. Tossing their bags on the bed, she rushed to the balcony taking in all of the sights and sounds below them. "Tis amazing, come see."

Stalls of vendors lined the road next to the canal.

Killian set Ameria on a cushioned chair behind him then leaned over the rail. "We should order room service and eat out here."

"That's a grand idea. I'll give the wee one a bath while ye order food?" She scooped up Ameria. "Come on, I'll create a bubble dolphin for ye again."

Isla glanced back at Killian as she walked inside. She could get used to this.

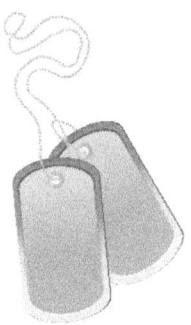

# Chapter Twenty-Three

K illian hung up the phone and blew out a deep breath.

Isla walked out on the balcony and handed him a coffee cup. "How was the call with yer parents?"

"Same as every other time. Mom asked when I'm coming home and Dad asked if I'm enlisting again. One thing for sure. Now that I'm officially out of the service, I'm getting my own place."

"I'm sorry, I wish ye had more supportive parents."

He reached his arms behind his back and stretched. Talking to his parents always made him tense. Sleeping next to Isla and not pulling her against him made the tension ten times worse. "What about your parents? You've never mentioned them."

"They weren't magical so they died a very long

time ago."

Killian choked on the sip of coffee he'd just swallowed. "I am so sorry. I should have realized that when you mentioned you hadn't gotten your magic from them."

She waved him off. "It was difficult for the first few decades but now they're just happy memories."

"But still, that must have been so hard for you."

She took a long sip of her tea before answering. "Tis exactly why I avoid humans at all costs. It's painful to get close to them then watch them age and pass on."

A knot formed in his stomach. He was human, which meant he had no shot with her and he really couldn't blame her. He'd been hoping she'd be interested in a relationship when this was over but now, he realized it was all a pipe dream. He was going to have to enjoy her for as long as she'd have him, then let her go.

The tension on the balcony was thick enough to suffocate him. "We've tried almost every restaurant on this street. There's one left, should we go get lunch?"

She blinked rapidly, her eyes wide. Was she trying to blink away tears? "Sounds good, I should probably get out of these pajama's anyway."

Brayan climbed up Killian and rested on his shoulder. He still didn't understand any noise that came from the familiar, but he was cute enough he didn't mind. "Don't worry, I'll get fish and share with you again."

The Stout nuzzled his nose against Killian's neck.

He held the door for Isla as they made their way out. The cafe was at the far end of the street. Over the last few days, they had only gone out long enough to grab some to-go food and a few groceries but this was the first time they were going to sit in a restaurant.

Killian stopped at a street vendor selling tulips and bought one for each of them. Ameria squealed when he handed her a yellow one.

Isla took a deep breath of the sweet scent. "You spoil us."

Killian shrugged, not wanting to make a big deal out of it.

The cafe's outdoor seating was only half full. Not many people wanted to brave eating outside even with the large heaters scattered around.

The young woman at the hostess stand called out a greeting. "Welcome. If you want inside seating it will be a bit before a table is ready. I can seat you outside immediately."

Killian turned toward Isla and let her make the decision.

She nodded to the girl. "Outside is fine, we don't mind the cold."

Killian held back a snort. Of course, the two magical creatures didn't mind. He on the other hand was taking the closest chair to the heater.

He thanked the hostess for the menu as he sat. "Ugh, it's not in English. Can you just order me a coke and the fish and chips or whatever fish dish they have?"

Isla rolled her eyes as she chuckled. "We have a lot of downtime. I think it's time ye start learning a new language. Which one do ye want to start with?"

The idea of trying to learn a new language was daunting but if it meant more time with her, he would take it. "Gaelic is your native tongue, right? We can start there?"

Her eyebrows shot up. "Are ye sure, that's one of the harder ones?"

"I have the best teacher in Ireland. It might take a lot of extra work but I'm sure she'll have me speaking it in no time." He winked at her.

Yipping from a nearby table had Ameria bouncing in Killian's lap. A small dog excitedly jumped in the air trying to get to the Princess. The older couple holding the leash tried unsuccessfully to shush the animal. "He's friendly if she wants to meet him."

Killian turned back to Isla. "I'm going to take her over to see the dog while you order."

His chair scraped across the ground as he slid back. The woman was frantically trying to get the spastic dog to settle down. "I'm so sorry, he's usually very calm."

Killian let Ameria stand. The dog immediately sat in front of her. She reached toward it and let it lick her face.

It wasn't long before Ameria was sitting on the

ground, the dog in her lap. Her giggles had everyone watching.

"Killian."

The hairs on the back of his neck went up. Isla's tone was not right. She pointed down the road to a group of women stopping everyone holding a baby or pushing a stroller and inspecting the children.

"Okay Ameria, it's time to go." He picked her up and walked quickly following Isla inside. She handed the waitress cash for the order they'd put in but hadn't gotten. Surprised faces followed them as they made their way through the kitchen and out the back door.

"We'll take the alleyway then cross over to the hotel."

"I couldn't see anything different about them, who were they?"

Isla's mouth formed a grim line. "Witches, and not the Glenda kind. I know every magic-user on this continent, so I recognize them."

His years of military service were a blessing at that moment. He felt no fear, only determination to get them safely back to their room and out of the area.

When it came time to cross the road, Isla sent Brayan out to see if the coven was close. "He doesn't see them, let's hurry across."

Killian wrapped his jacket around Ameria as tightly as possible trying to hide her from view. Lucky for them he was a big man and shielded her easily.

They got to the room safely, rushing to pack everything.

Killian held the door open for Isla then scanned the room to make sure they had everything. Ameria's plant sat on the bedside table. If they had left that there would have been hell to pay. "That would have been a nightmare."

Brayan ran ahead, darting around people who couldn't see him. Isla held her hand up to stop him at the lobby entrance. "Hang on, he's checking around the car."

Killian kept his breath steady as they waited. "Okay, he saw them go in a shop. We have to make it fast."

He tossed her the keys when they got close. "Turn on the car and keep your head down. I'll get Ameria strapped in then drive down the road while you stay hidden."

Killian kept his heartbeat steady as he got Ameria in the car and went around to drive. Isla stayed slumped in the seat as they turned down the road and made their way out of the city.

"You can get up now, we're clear." Killian turned on the GPS. "So, where are we headed next?"

"Bruges is an hour away. I'll see if I can get us a room. I think we should circle around for a bit when we get there to see if we can spot any patrols."

Twelve more days, they had to keep it together for twelve more days then Ameria would be halfway across the world. Killian prayed that would throw everyone off her scent since they'd been searching so hard in Europe. He looked in the rearview mirror at Ameria. So young to have so much violence and grief thrust upon her. He was determined to make her life the best it could be for the next twelve days he had with her.

# Chapter Twenty-Four

Isla sat on the balcony of their new hotel room watching the sunrise shimmer on the water of the canal below.

Except for meals delivered by room service, they stayed locked in the room. Brayan patrolled the hotel twice a day and so far, everything had been quiet.

They spent their time watching TV and entertaining the Princess who was desperate to walk on her own but not quite there yet.

Isla's phone was full of pictures, documenting their time with her. The longer they stayed cooped up, the more she rambled in Ameria's journal.

Now four days after arriving she was frustrated and awake at the break of dawn. She hoped the sunlight would recharge her like it did at home.

The door to the balcony slid open quietly. Killian poked his head out. "Everything okay?"

Isla sighed as she stared off in the distance. "Aye, I'm missing the forest and the cliffs. I hate being so cooped up."

He pushed the door wider and came out with the comforter from the bed wrapped around him. "Christ on a cracker it's cold out here. Can you spare a little magical heat for me?"

Honestly, she hadn't even realized she'd been keeping herself warm with her magic. It had become second nature. "We can't have ye turning into a popsicle now can we."

He pulled a chair close to her. She knew the second he entered the bubble of warmth because he sighed and relaxed his shoulders. "You know if you want a little break, we could take a ride on the canal. Go first thing before most of the tourists are up then be back in here for the day?"

She knew it was a risk but the idea of getting out even for an hour was too good to pass up. Between her and Killian they could handle anything that came their way.

They took turns showering and dressing, both eager for Ameria to wake so they could go.

When the Princess was finally awake, fed, and changed, they made their way out of the hotel. You'd think they were going to Disney Land in Paris, they were that excited.

Isla held Ameria close as they walked the short distance to one of the tour operators. She was grateful to only see two other families and an older couple waiting in line.

Killian leaned close and whispered. "They all look human to me, what about you?"

She nodded. "Aye, run of the mill humans."

"Wow, make us sound so boring."

She stuck her tongue out at him as she handed her ticket to the captain and boarded the boat.

They took seats at the back of the boat so everyone would be in front of them. Ameria stood on the seat and pressed her face against the window.

Isla cracked the window to allow some of the fresh air in. The smell of the sea calmed her.

Ten minutes into the tour they heard something hitting the bottom and sides of the boat. The gray-haired captain stopped talking and leaned over the edge. "I've never seen anything like it." He turned back to the group, grinning from ear to ear. "I'm not sure what has the fish all riled up but we're surrounded. It's been years since I've seen this many in the canal at one time. Have a look."

Ameria squealed as a fish jumped in the air and smacked against her window.

Isla jumped. "Shite, they're attacking."

Killian shook his head. "I don't think so. I think they're just trying to be close to her."

Murmurs all around the boat rose as the fish got more and more excited.

Isla held her hand out and created several closed roses. "Ameria, look, I have something for ye to play with." She thrust the flowers toward the Princess hoping to distract her.

Ameria gave her a toothless smile as she

grabbed the buds and sat on the bench. After a few seconds, the thumping quieted down.

Killian let out a deep breath. "Phew, I was getting a little nervous."

"She makes every day an adventure, doesn't she?" Isla hadn't thought about being a parent in decades. Spending this time with Ameria and Killian had her questioning everything. Tears burned in her eyes as she thought about their time coming to an end.

Killian wrapped his arm around her shoulders. "What's going on in your head right now?"

"I was thinking about how hard it was going to be to give her up. Now I understand why the Council demanded we each only have her for one month. As much as I miss me cottage, I have to admit it's going to be painful when it's time to say goodbye."

Killian's head rested on top of hers. "I've been thinking a lot about that, too. These have truly been the best three weeks of my life. It's going to be tough saying goodbye but I know we have to."

"What about us? When our month is up, are we as well?" She hated the crack she heard in her voice.

He squeezed her hand. "I already told you you're stuck with me if you want to be. I have to show you the sights of America, remember?"

She nodded without looking up at him. If they survived the next seven days, she was definitely going to take him up on his offer.

# Chapter Twenty-Five

After their adventure on the canal boat two days earlier, they'd decided it was best to stay locked away until they were ready to move locations again. Killian really didn't mind. There was so much to learn about the supernatural world. They'd spent hours talking about the various creatures and what lore was or wasn't true about them. He'd been bummed to find out leprechauns weren't friendly little guys who loved rainbows. Apparently, they had razor-sharp teeth, were greedy assholes, and loved to make deals with people but made sure it was stated in a way that they always came out on top.

"Morning, look who's bright-eyed and bushy-tailed." Isla walked out on the balcony holding Ameria. The Princess smiled at him coyly from under Isla's chin.

Killian leaned forward and spread out the blanket they kept out there so Isla could put Ameria down to play. Isla created several wooden building blocks for her to play with.

Several squeaks came from the hotel room as Brayan came running out. He loved the toys more than Ameria did. Their favorite game was the Princess stacking them and Brayan knocking them over.

Four rapid bangs echoed down the road below them. Fear engulfed Killian, without thought he leaped on top of Ameria and covered her. His body so tense it was painful. Images from the IED explosion flooded his mind.

A gentle touch on his back had him curling even tighter. "Killian, it's okay. Those weren't gunshots. Come on, let Ameria go. We're safe."

It took a full minute for his brain to accept her words. He sat up, cold wind hit his face and he realized he had tears rolling down his cheeks. "I'm sorry. Certain noises really trigger me."

Isla held her hand out and helped him up. "I'm grateful you were clear-headed enough to think to protect Ameria." She pointed at a truck stopped down the road. "It was a delivery truck backfiring."

He was mortified. He hadn't had an episode in three weeks and had hoped to get out of this without one. He wasn't ashamed of his PTSD. Therapy had helped him see that he had been through something horrific and it was his mind's way of working through it. Don't tell that to his dad though, he thought it was a load of bullshit and mocked Killian for it whenever it was brought up.

"I'll get you some coffee." He sat back down as Isla retreated into the room. Would she think less of him now?

He kept his eyes down, watching Ameria who had thought the whole thing had been a game.

Isla held the cup in front of his face.

"Thanks." He was afraid to see pity in her eyes.

Her phone on the small table next to his chair vibrated loudly against the glass top.

She sat next to him and put the phone on speaker. "Nic, how's it going?"

The girl on the other end snorted. "I should be asking you that. How's nanny duty going?"

"It's really not as horrible as ye think. As long as ye know a spell to block yer sense of smell and yer gag reflex isn't too bad, ye should be fine."

"Delightful. I can't wait."

Killian heard the sarcasm in the other mage's voice.

"At least I have five more days of freedom."

Isla rolled her eyes. "I think all of ye are worrying too much. The Princess is a dream to take care of."

Killian tilted his head to the side as he stared at Isla. Had the two of them been taking care of the same baby?

"I don't even need to use magic to know you're full of shit. But that's not why I called. The Council wants to check-in and see the Princess is okay. They agreed to only send my father and I trust him completely. There's no way he's the assassin."

Killian didn't like it but he had no say.

Isla pursed her lips as she thought for a second. "We're in Bruges, I'll send ye the address."

"How the hell did you end up in Belgium?"

"Hey, we're on the run. Everywhere we go, there's hunting parties looking for us."

"Does that mean the hot as fuck human is still with you? Have you screwed him yet?"

Killian slapped his hand over his mouth to keep his laughter quiet.

Isla closed her eyes and shook her head. "You're on speaker... he's with me now."

There was silence for a few seconds. "I guess that answers my first question. I still want to know the second answer."

"Goodbye, Nic."

"By the way, I haven't told my father about your man."

"Ugh, thanks for that."

Nic laughed as the call disconnected.

"Shite." Isla aggressively pushed the end call button.

Killian cleared his throat. "Should I hide while he's here?"

"Absolutely not. Yer as valuable to the mission as I am."

Not that it mattered to the council. They were going to be pissed when they found out a human was taking care of their precious royal.

He took a sip of coffee. "So, you think I'm hot?"

She scowled at him. "I'm going to start packing. Once her dad knows where we are, I want to move on. She may trust him but he's still a Druid Elf and I'm still responsible for Ameria."

"You're the boss. Let's get started."

The woodblocks disintegrated as Isla bent down to pick Ameria up. "Come on, I'll give ye more blocks to play with in the crib while we get everything ready."

They'd moved so many times they were professionals now. As they zipped the last bag closed, there was a knock on the door. Killian picked up Ameria. He wanted her close in case anything happened.

Isla looked through the peephole of the door before opening it and letting an older man with a full head of white hair inside. His long, green robes definitely would have him standing out among humans.

The Elf leaned forward and kissed each of Isla's cheeks. "I hope you are well?"

"Klaus, it's good to see ye. I heard yer still having a lot of unrest?"

The older man nodded then stopped short when he noticed Killian and Ameria. His face shifted from friendly to angry in an instant. "Who's this?"

Isla moved to stand between them. "This is Killian. He's human and has saved yer Princess's life multiple times over the last three weeks. Her highness also took a liking to him immediately upon meeting him. He has been an invaluable help to me."

He pursed his lips as he studied Killian. "Fine but I will need to report this to the Council."

Isla nodded. "That's not a problem. I trust him with me life and the life of the Princess."

"Very well." He didn't seem appeased but dropped the subject. "I was sent to see for myself that her Highness was well and to give you an update. We're still scouring the Kingdom. We've interrogated hundreds thus far with no credible information." He walked close to Killian and studied Ameria. Did he think they were hurting her? "We weren't pleased how fast word spread of the assassination. A few lesser intelligent beings have tried to infiltrate our walls but our Army has kept them at bay."

"I know the mages wouldn't have spread the word. It would seem yer walls have more than a few leaks."

Klaus sneered at Isla. Killian wasn't sure she should be prodding him so aggressively.

"You worry about the Princess and we'll worry about our leaks." He made a motion with his hands. Colors appeared like a swirling vortex right in the center of the room. He stopped before entering the portal. "I'm sorry, you can imagine what a stressful time this is. I don't mean to be so curt. I wish you well."

He stepped through the vortex and disappeared.

"Okay, now that was cool. How come you didn't

have swirly colors when you transported us?"

Isla picked up the bags off the bed. "Different magic has different outcomes."

He grabbed Ameria's plant off the table. "His is pretty cool." He knew he was playing with fire but he wanted to lighten the mood.

She tossed Ameria's jacket at his head. "Next time we have to portal, I'll make sure not to take ye with me in me ugly one."

He grabbed his chest like he was wounded. "Ouch, you would just leave me behind?"

She glanced over her shoulder at him before walking out the door of their room. "Offend me magic again and find out."

# Chapter Twenty-Six

I sla jumped awake when she heard the hotel door open. She instantly created a sword, ready to fight the intruder.

Killian held his hands up, a bag in one hand, a tray of drinks in the other. "It's just me, I went down to get some breakfast."

Isla groaned as she flopped back against her pillow. "Ugh, what time is it?"

Killian glanced at the alarm clock on the bedside table. "Five-Thirty."

"In the morning? Why are ye up at this hour?"

He set the food down quietly. "I couldn't sleep." He walked over to the bed holding his phone out. "Which turned out great because it gave me a lot of time to read up on Amsterdam. There's a place we need to go after Ameria's up."

It had been completely dark when they'd driven in the night before. Isla had been hoping to see some of the city before they moved on again. "I'm guessing ye were the kid who got his parents up in the middle of the night on Christmas morning aren't ye? I'm excited to see the city, too, but I didn't stay up all night waiting to go." Isla loved teasing him, he was easy to rile up.

"I didn't stay up out of excitement. I just couldn't sleep." He handed her a to-go cup. Steam was still escaping around the lid. "Since you're up now, want to watch the sunrise together?"

That had always been a solitary ritual of hers. Not that others couldn't enjoy the sunrise, but did they get the same sense of invigoration out of it that she did? She always felt exposed the moments before the sun peeked over the horizon. Was she ready to be so vulnerable with another person?

She ran her fingers through her hair before grabbing the cup. "Sounds lovely. Let me use the restroom and I'll meet ye on the balcony."

The bright light of the bathroom nearly blinded her. "Ah Jaaaysus. Can't they put a dimmer switch in here?"

She normally wasn't cranky in the mornings but she had a lot of pent-up sexual tension after sharing a bed with Killian for the past two weeks so she wasn't getting the best sleep.

The hot cup of tea waiting for her wasn't going to taste very good but she had to brush her teeth. She lifted her arm and jerked back. "Shite, where's my deodorant."

Once she was semi-presentable, she peeked in

on the sleeping Princess before going out on the balcony. "I wish I could sleep as well as she does."

Killian nodded, his eyes wide. "Can you imagine if she had sleeping issues on top of everything else? We definitely would be in over our heads then."

The familiar orange glow of the sky caught her attention. She leaned on the rail, her arms crossed like she was hugging herself.

Killian must have understood her ritual. He stayed quietly in his chair and let her have her moment.

When she couldn't stare at the bright light any longer, she closed her eyes and tilted her head back.

"God, you're gorgeous. You're glowing in the sunlight."

A compliment is always nice. Hearing it from Killian sent a shiver down her back. She turned to make a joke and found him inches from her. He put a hand on either side of her, trapping her. "I know I'm not what you want but I'm finding it hard to stay away from you."

He may not be what she wanted but he's definitely what she needed. Words were too messy, their lives were too messy but she couldn't resist him a second longer. Using the rail, she pushed herself up as tall as she could go and captured his mouth. To say he was shocked was an understatement. He froze not reacting to her lips against his. The awkwardness grew until she was about to pull away when he wrapped his arms around her and pulled her against him.

Electricity ran through her body. He tasted heavenly and his tongue knew exactly what to do. He trailed kisses down her neck. It was the single most fantastical mistake of her life.

Now that she'd crossed the line, could she go back?

Ameria's babble broke the spell. He stepped away, their chests rising and falling rapidly. He crossed his hands behind his head and tried taking deep breaths to regain control.

Isla didn't know what to say so she escaped. "I'm sorry." She skirted around him and went inside. "Good Morning Princess. Let's get ye changed then some breakfast."

While she cleaned Ameria up and put fresh clothes on her, Isla tried to ignore Killian walking around behind her. She thought she had been aware of him before. Now everything was hyper-focused. The idea of sleeping next to him later gave her heartburn. When things settled down, and they were done with their mission, they needed to have a long talk about whether they could have a casual relationship or if he was going to need more than that.

A voice in the back of her mind was screaming that she wanted more but she shut that voice up quickly. It was too complicated with a human.

"I have a bottle ready. I'll take her so you can get showered and changed."

How could he sound so normal and unaffected

when she still felt like her insides were liquid? "Aye, thanks."

A long, hot shower would go a long way to calm her raging hormones. If it didn't, she was going to have to take another shower after everyone went to sleep and try to get him out of her system.

Isla gasped as their destination came into view.

Killian swept his arm in a wide arc. "I present to you, The Floating Flower Market."

The canal was littered with barges moored to the side. They were set up as shops they could walk on and off of. Tulips of every color spilled out of the stores. Ameria squealed and reached her arm out squeezing her hand open and closed. "Are you sure we can control her here?"

Killian held Ameria up in front of his face. "I know you love flowers, and we've given you some everywhere we went. If you want to see all the pretty flowers you need to act human. This means no using your magic on any of the flowers."

"Or the fish in the canal," Isla interjected.

Killian nodded. "Right, I don't know if you understand me but I'm asking you not to do any magic here, okay?"

Ameria's bright green eyes studied Killian then Isla before she turned back to Killian and smiled broadly, drool running down her chin. Isla had no idea how to interpret that response. She didn't think Ameria actually understood but when they needed her calm during desperate situations she always seemed to understand.

Killian settled Ameria back on his hip and leaned toward Isla. "I'll defer to you. We can stay or we can go?"

The various stalls with flowers, cheese, and wine were calling to her. "We can take a short walk through."

Isla felt like they were walking on eggshells. Each table of flowers they passed they watched closely to see if they moved toward Ameria. They leaned toward her as if blowing in the wind but nothing a human would look twice at.

Various vendors called out, offering samples of their goods. They filled a bag with chocolates and cheese, each vendor gushing over their beautiful family.

Killian pointed at a boat up ahead. "I'm freezing, can we grab a coffee?"

"Sorry, I forget how much more sensitive you are."

"I'm not going to respond to that. I have zero toxic masculinity. One of my commanders was a woman and she was the bravest woman I'd ever met. She could also kick my ass with one arm tied behind her back."

"Ye don't talk much about yer time in the military."

They moved forward in the coffee line, waiting

their turn. "It's a habit to bury it all down deep where my father can't exploit it. But honestly, we had a lot of good times, too."

"Ye should never forget yer friend," She pointed toward the dog tag around his neck. "But if ye want a chance at happiness ye need to try to focus on more of the good times than the bad."

"You know, you're pretty wise for your age."

"You don't live two hundred years without learning a thing or two."

Killian snorted. "I honestly forgot about that. You look younger than me."

She elbowed his side gently. "I'm prettier, too."

He turned to face her, his smile gone. "You are fucking gorgeous."

"De volgende," The tiny woman behind the counter waved them forward.

Before Isla could interject Killian held out his phone. "Spreek je engels?" His attempt at Dutch was horrendous.

The older woman smiled happily. "I do, thank you for trying my language before just assuming."

Killian slid his phone back in his jacket pocket. "I'd like a coffee with cream, and she'll have..."

He trailed off waiting for her to answer. "Tea with milk please."

"Of course, one moment."

Killian glanced at Ameria. "Can babies have hot chocolate?"

Isla shrugged. "I have the small list Kleo made for us and that's not on there so I'm not risking it."

The woman returned and set the to-go cups down. "Oh no, what happened." She rushed around the counter to one of the shelves on the side. Packets of tulip seeds had ripped open, roots and sprouts were sticking out. "I don't understand, there's no soil or water."

Killian and Isla grimaced as they looked at Ameria. The Princess chewed on her finger as she watched the commotion.

Isla threw more than enough money on the counter and pulled Killian out of there. "Let's grab her a flower and get back to the hotel. That was enough exploring for one day."

Four more days, they just had to stay under the radar for four more days.

# Chapter Twenty-Seven

"**A**msterdam has been my favorite hideout location so far."

Killian nodded. "It has been a nice couple of days. Hopefully, we can finish out the month here."

Isla leaned over the rail of the canal and watched a boat go by. "If we move again, we're heading to Germany next. I think we've pushed our luck for long enough in this country." She sighed happily. Killian should have been looking at the sights around them but he couldn't see past her. She stood up and started walking again. "I don't say this lightly when I say Amsterdam might be just as beautiful as Ireland."

Killian looked around the canal street. "The colors of the flowers everywhere are beautiful but too many people for me. I enjoyed the peacefulness of the cliffs. I had a gorgeous view every morning."

Her face pinkened.

He opened his mouth to say more when he saw two men across the street watching them. The hairs on the back of his neck stood up. They were some kind of supernatural creature, but he didn't know what kind.

He turned toward the water and pointed at a building across the canal. "I think we're being followed. Act like we're looking at something so I can see if there are more than the two I spotted."

His stomach dropped when he saw ten more closing in on them. "Let's get into that alley and you'll have to portal us back to the room."

Isla grabbed his hand and walked quickly toward the alley ahead.

Killian knew it was a mistake the second they turned. There were already men waiting for them. Isla went back to back with Killian so they could keep an eye on the growing number of people coming at them from both sides.

"What are they, I can't tell?" A tall man with stringy black hair hissed at him. Sharp pointed teeth protruded from his mouth. "Never mind, I'm guessing those are vampires. I thought they only had two fangs, that looks like a whole lot more." He knew he was rambling but, in his defense, it was the first time ever seeing a real-life vampire.

Isla whispered words behind him. Two large mud creatures appeared in front of him. "Get them." They rushed at the few vampires that had been in the alleyway. Isla and Killian ran through them trying to get further away from the larger group behind them. They just needed enough time for Isla to transport them.

A scream echoed down the corridor. Killian spun to see what new fresh hell was waiting for them.

Isla had conjured three more mud monsters who were trying to push back the larger group. Thrashing above them explained the scream. Vines that had been growing down the side of the building had pulled one of the vamps up. Killian shuddered as he watched the ropes squeeze him tight against the wall. Only one person could be doing that. Ameria squirmed in his arms, giggling as she watched the vines moving. "Bloodthirsty little thing, aren't you?" One of the monsters sent a vampire hurtling in the air. "I could really use that gun right about now."

Isla shook her head, concentrating on her creations. "Bullets don't hurt them." She let out a scream as one of the mud monsters was overrun by vampires.

Killian grabbed her arm. "It hurts you when they get hurt?"

Sweat poured down her face. "Aye, they're connected to me."

A tiny woman broke through the line. "Our master knows you're here. There's more coming and you can't stop us."

Killian grabbed Isla's hand. "Teleport us now, not back to the hotel just somewhere." He knew what he was asking. The amount of magical energy she had already used meant traveling might not work but they had to try.

The wave of nausea hit him as they disappeared from the alley.

As they landed, he bent over, still holding tight to Ameria trying to keep from throwing up again.

"We made it." Isla's breathy declaration was the last thing she said before passing out. Killian caught her with his free arm.

"Shit." He glanced around trying to take in the room around him. The walls were covered in tiny pictures. He was relieved the words were in English. He was not ready to use Google translator for German.

A buzzing sound behind him abruptly stopped. His head snapped around. A gorgeous woman with long sapphire blue hair and more tattoos than Isla had stood up and walked toward him. "I'm guessing you're the hot as fuck American?"

# Chapter Twenty-Eight

Isla felt like concrete was poured on top of her keeping her pinned down. Confusion muddled her brain until the memories of the alley fight with the golems and vampires came rushing back. She bolted upright. "Ameria."

The door of the dimly lit room swung open. Killian hurried in with the Princess in his arms. "Thank god. Nic said you were fine but it's been eighteen hours."

Isla pushed herself up against the headboard of the bed. "So, we made it? I wasn't really sure I had enough power left to get us here."

"Amsterdam to New Orleans with them in tow was impressive." Nic stood in the doorway, a plate in her hand. "You're a day early and you're lucky I was only tattooing myself when you dropped in." She set the food down on the bedside table. "In all seriousness though, I'm glad you made it out safe. It sounds like it got tense there for a minute."

Ameria squirmed in Killian's arms and reached for Isla. Killian looked as surprised as she did. The Princess immediately wrapped her arms around Isla's neck and hugged her. Tears sprang to her eyes. Did she understand they had almost died?

"I'll grab you a drink." Killian walked out, leaving them alone.

Nic sat on the edge of the bed. "I had Morwen clean out your hotel room. Your shit is here." She pointed to their bags in the corner of the room. "So, really, how was it? Is this going to be the worst month of my life?"

Isla stared at the door Killian had walked through. "It was the best time I've had in centuries. And that includes the time the Guild got drunk during the Winter Solstice celebration and almost blew up half of Paris." She turned tear-filled eyes to her friend. "I think I'm in love and that really sucks."

Nic's face scrunched in confusion. "I would think you were an idiot if you weren't in love with him. I'm jealous actually. I hope I stumble on some fine ass man willing to give up his life for a month to protect a woman and a child he doesn't know."

When she put it like that Isla couldn't argue.

Killian came back with a bottle of water and a hot cup of tea.

Isla tilted her head studying him. "Do you want to keep the sight permanently? I know ye've seen a lot so I don't blame ye if ye want to forget all of this."

Killian took his time looking at each of them. "No matter what happens next, I don't want to go back to not knowing."

Killian stood by the window staring down at the Celtic knot tattooed over his heart. Isla had branded him physically and emotionally and he was all for it.

"I'm going to get ye." Isla pretended to attack Ameria's neck. The child pulled her shoulders up, giggling as she pushed at Isla's face.

"So, what happens now? Nic's month has officially started."

Isla straightened up and chewed her lip. "I think I remember something about ye giving me a tour of America?"

"How about we fly up to Chicago so my parents can see I'm still alive then we'll go from there?"

Isla turned white, which was impressive given how pale she already was. "I'm not getting on a plane."

Killian's mouth opened and closed then opened again. "You'll teleport, take the Chunnel, and ferry across large bodies of water but you won't fly? Have you ever been on a plane?"

She shook her head aggressively. "No, why would I when I can teleport wherever I want to go? Ye give me the location and I'll portal us there."

"No way, you aren't draining yourself again so soon. Just because we won't have Ameria anymore doesn't mean they will stop looking for you." He crossed his arms over his chest. "What did you tell me, oh yeah, I won't let anything happen to you while we're hurtling through the air."

He knew he had her. She made him do a lot of crazy shit, she could handle one quick plane ride.

She handed Ameria to him and grabbed their bags. They found Nic in the tattoo parlor.

Isla stopped and reached back to take her necklace off. She clipped it around Ameria's neck. She held up the small gold charm hanging from it. "This is a Claddaugh. I want ye to think of us whenever ye look at it. Ye have a tough road ahead but know that we love ye and wish ye well."

Killian swiped a tear from Isla's cheek. "This isn't goodbye forever. We'll see her again soon." He sounded more confident than he felt. He hadn't met the other ten mages but he prayed they were as good as Isla was and Nic seemed to be.

Isla took a deep breath and wiped her face. "Yer right. We'll see each other again before ye know it."

Killian's stomach was in knots as he hugged Ameria and passed her off to Isla.

Isla walked toward Nic as if she was walking to

her death. She kissed Ameria on the cheek. "Be well Your Highness."

Nic's lip curled slightly as she took the baby. "I still can't believe we agreed to this shit. Keep your phone on. I'll call you if she does something I don't know how to handle."

Isla grabbed a book out of her bag. "Read the memory book. I journaled our time together and all the mistakes we made with her. But call me any time. I want regular updates knowing ye guys are safe."

Killian cleared his throat. Unshed tears burning his eyes.

Isla held her hand out to him. "Nic said we have to try a beignet before we go to the airport."

Killian held the door open for her. "Whatever you say. This is your vacation."

He knew it was so much more than that though. He'd gone to Ireland to heal his PTSD and instead found himself *Mated to a Mage*.

## The End

Isla and Killian will be back in 2022 with a whole new mage adventure.

Ameria's story continues with Nic in the book *Mage You Blink* by Gracen Miller is now available. You can pre-order all of the books now.

Cassidy K. O'Connor

Join the Nightshade Guild fan group at
https://www.facebook.com/nightshadeguild

# ~Other Books by the Author~

### Raven's Haven Series
Fighting For Forgiveness

Sassy Mates: In My Mate's Sight
Sassy Mates: In My Mate's Defense

Paranormal Dating Agency: My Oath To You

### Stand Alones
Broken Dreams
The Laird's Promise
Sexy In White
Forever Yours, Casey
To Steal a Prince's Heart
Wicked Wonderland Retreat Box Set
Her Royal Choice: A Reverse Harem Romance

### The Love's Protector Series
Tempted by the Fae
Seduced by the Fae
Charmed by the Fae
Healed by the Fae
**Redeemed by the Fae**

### Black Hollow Series
Reviving Love
Sacrificing Love
Accepting Love
Resisting Love

# ABOUT THE AUTHOR

Cassidy K. O'Connor is a born and raised Floridian who loves to travel but never forgets where her roots are. She married her high school sweetheart, they have 3 kids, and a dog she is obsessed with. Travelling and reading are her two favorite hobbies. Cassidy loves all things Ireland and has been lucky enough to visit twice. Her dream is to watch a baseball game in every MLB stadium in the country.

Books by Cassidy typically involve independent, strong, female main characters and equally strong men who pursue them.

To learn more about Cassidy please visit her online at www.cassidykoconnor.com.

You can also find her on Facebook at www.facebook.com/cassidykoconnorauthor

She always welcomes new friends and encourages readers to reach out to her.

www.ingramcontent.com/pod-product-compliance
Lightning Source LLC
Chambersburg PA
CBHW060223180626
46813CB00007B/2945